JADED DIAMOND

JADED DIAMOND

A journey out of the darkness and into the light

Penny D. Burnham

Soul Castle Books Inc.

JADED DIAMOND
Copyright © 2013 by Penny D. Burnham

Published by Soul Castle Books Inc.
www.soulcastlebooks.com

All rights reserved. This book may not be reproduced in whole or in part without written permission from the publisher.

This book is a work of fiction. Names, characters, businesses, places, events and incidents either are a product of the author's imagination or are used fictitiously. Any resemblance to actual persons, living or dead, events or locales is entirely coincidental.

ISBN 978-1-927635-00-1

First Edition
Printed in Canada

For all who seek

JADED

adj. worn out by overwork or abuse;
tired or dulled through repetition or excess;
lacking or losing spirit because something
has been experienced too many times;
wearied; cynical; pretentiously callous

JADE

n. a sacred gemstone, revered for its strength,
efficacy and beauty

ONE

Security is mostly a superstition. It does not exist in nature, nor do the children of men as a whole experience it. Avoiding danger is no safer in the long run than outright exposure. Life is either a daring adventure or nothing.

—Helen Keller

I have spent the majority of my life in the dark, mostly alone and usually with a drink in one hand. When I refer to the dark, I don't mean literally. When I say a drink, I mean a Bombay Sapphire rocks with a twist.

In reality, at least what most would consider real, I live a very public life, where being pretty is an advantage. People lie to get what they want and I pretend that I trust every single one of them. The truth is, I hate people and have been personally choking the life out of myself for as long as I can remember. I live days, months, years at a time, secretively longing to slit someone's throat rather than smile. I am speaking figuratively, of course, but endlessly do find myself sitting in a room full of people with only a grim, empty smirk, pretending everything is fine, and doing my damnedest to convince even myself.

Haunted by this polite and perpetual need of mine to be kind to those unable to handle the real truth, I find myself *managing* my life rather than living it, covering rather than caring. Although not apparent from the outside, an inner insatiability accompanies this kind of life, whereby needs are never quite met, where fixing takes precedence over feeling, and where the lingering rewards of all that you do are merely reminders you've never done quite enough. Incessantly and often unconsciously, however, you learn to survive each day by faking your sincerity, operating as a professional and leaving all to believe that you have handled their interests with the utmost care, only to go home and sedate yourself with a tall, stiff drink, or six.

So I exaggerate, or then again maybe I don't, but that is not to say that self-medicating is not necessary from time to time, in order for me to maintain my tight-lipped tolerance. I'm referring to those particular situations—and you know the people I mean—where even one less second of their insufferable story might have left you even somewhat interested, but instead you are left only irritated and enraged.

Left over any length of time, your clever facade soon begins to exist on a continuum where your public and private passions are drastic opposites, creating a world filled with chaos and confusion, giving you yet one more reason to numb yourself as protection from the insanity. You are not alone in this. The world is full of those who are emotionally frozen and out of touch with what they really want. People choose to please rather than pursue, abandoning their real dreams because they are too busy tolerating, rather than taking the time to focus and excel. For the most part, there are thousands out there just like you, and yet you feel alone, separate and selfish for wanting even a small part for yourself. You learn to ignore those inner desires that ignite you and grind on, assuming and accepting that it is now your sole responsibility to bear burden, so that others may in turn render fruit. My only question is, Who the hell told you that, and why did you listen?

So many of us have listened, however, causing us to evolve into an entire planet of people tormented by the very dreams that should be giving us joy; and secretively, we continue to hold each other captive in this unspoken global agreement of denial. This is not to say I condemn this type of tunnel existence—it does serve a purpose in certain realms. As far as effectiveness goes, it does well on the work front, and certainly provides success for me in my business life, although not a great deal of personal satisfaction. With this particular lifestyle, however, I tend to develop a set of driven and destructive behaviours that I choose to participate in routinely, if not daily, and a long line of dysfunctional relationships that I discard when I am edged too close to any self-discovery.

It is not the life I expected for myself.

∞∞∞∞∞∞∞∞

I suppose no one ever expects to end up living a lie. The thing about lies, however, is this: Until you know a larger truth, until you have a bigger perspective from which to look, they are real, and the fact that you are under any type of illusion is not even an option you consider. Essentially, you can lie to yourself every single day without knowledge. My story is one such case. This hatred that I harboured as such a defining truism for myself, I would more than humbly come to discover, held no actual trace of reality in the outside world.

If there is one truth I now know to be certain, it is that you must uncover your own hidden agendas. Until you start looking for them and muster the courage to dig deeply, you have no idea of the twisted and tormented excuses for reality that you actually live by; and as the common cliché goes, the truth will out, often emerging from the very last place you might have expected to look.

∞∞∞∞∞∞∞∞

Mozart plays quietly in the background as I sit at my antique executive desk and stare at the mound of manuscripts that still lies before me, begging for attention like neglected middle children. His famous *Requiem* is my favourite. Authentically performed on period instruments, its melody provides the harmony I require for my work, while its rapture, oscillating between chaos and contentment, helps inspire me to greatness. I have always needed the extremes to excel.

I once read somewhere that it is not the typical and familiar in Mozart's work that captures the imagination, but the untypical and unfamiliar. And it's true. The challenge is in the ability to hear it. Like anything else, the message is there, but so too is the resistance to its sound, similar to a room with a view on an overcast day, I think as I look out the window and onto the ocean below. A smile edges out of hiding when I realize it is a clear night in the city. I remember how annoyed I was when I was looking for this place and first heard the precise description of it that now runs through my mind.

∞∞∞∞∞∞∞∞∞

"On a clear day you have a view."
"Pardon?"
"On a clear day . . . you have a view."
"Uh . . . ?" I uttered, in my greatest attempt to be polite, while simultaneously wondering what the hell the realtor was talking about.
"You have a view."

What ever happened to a simple, straightforward answer? I remember thinking at the time as I silently fumed. What was wrong with people? You either have a view or do not have a view. Weather conditions can possibly obstruct the clarity of such a view, but the view is a constant. It's either there or it's not. Several of the eccentrics who paraded me through many of the city's complexes, however, did hold their varied and imprecise opinions on a number of fundamentals, as I had discovered frustratingly first-hand. All I wanted was a place downtown, spacious with an office and a view. I did not want to waste time or money in senseless meetings. If the place did not have these basic elements, I was simply not interested. I did not need to be manipulated into situations that only held these qualities on a part-time basis or when the clouds were clear, or the moon was right. It was either all, or nothing. Success was a yes or no answer for me.

∞∞∞∞∞∞∞∞∞∞

Now overlooking my high-rise view twelve years later, I sit and smile at myself. I have not only become accustomed to people's quirky descriptions, but I, too, have developed the same muddled language for myself. And it is true—it's a clear night and I have a view.

It's amazing, I think as I look back now, how such a small fragment of conversation can become the precursor that defines a dozen years of life, and how quick we are to miss a simple lesson when our goal is to be right, rather than to learn. Like a room with a view, it's important to remember, all the essentials are continually present, but one has to wait until the clouds have cleared to enjoy the beauty. One has to trust that all that is required exists, even in times of complete disbelief. One has to believe, even in the face of no evidence, or of way too much.

As much of this faith as I have attempted to funnel into work lately, I have been searching for several months now for an answer I can't seem to find. As senior acquiring editor, this discovery is more important than just the satisfaction of a job well done at the end of the day. I need to find it. It's my responsibility and I'm certainly not giving up, but so far, nothing of any significance has surfaced. I am left ashamed, with no valid excuse for why I am an absolute failure on this project, and I have only myself to blame. And that fact is as black and distinct as the ink on the pages in front of me as I sit at home, alone again, reading book proposals.

    Pushing aside the manuscript that I have just finished reading, I reach for the next. I swear this package is my forty-second attempt tonight. Lifting the jacket cover of the proposal, I read, "*The Dancer*, by Jasmine Dubois." With a handful of tainted hope and only a single bucket of stubborn determination remaining, I dampen the corner of the page and lift, praying for release. Having no idea of the journey on which I am about to embark, or that it even exists out there as a possibility, I smooth my hand over the opening scene, and begin.

> Until their introduction, the idea of sexual adventure had left her void of any appetite. She envisioned saliva drooling from the mouth of a diseased dog, its fangs gnawing at her spirit in anticipation of its fulfillment, a raging rabid animal that would poison her indefinitely. And then one day, she decided love would no longer be evil.
>
> She would be no longer imprisoned by societal constraint or by the immature and underdeveloped intellect of those who preceded her. She would become a dancing gypsy, alive and free to escape the judgmental jealousy of all that was proper, and discard her familial contempt like an old ballet slipper, realizing its support had been sufficient in her formative years, but its cloth had worn bare and no longer served its purpose. She would begin to listen to the music that was rising from within. Its melodic flamenco strum would lead her into a

new song. And then one day, she would become who she had always been.

A true spirit, a wild woman, her glare was all encompassing and deadly. As she pranced with her painted toes pointed forward, their redness reminded him that she was the forbidden fruit, and ready for adventure. With her eyes pressed closed and the tips of her long lashes barely touching, her naked body and her long dark hair swayed to create a long line of lingering dreaminess as she transformed the negative space around them.

The beat quickened, causing a natural briskness of motion that made his heart knock from the inside outward. Pounding, pounding, watching, wanting a journey of the soul, a confidence of true identity . . .

Adjusting our criteria in the past few months, we have been recently looking for stories built on discovery, with characters real in their struggles, and authors who can create them. Our new identity, I guess you could say. What I want to find are journeys of personal liberation, where lives are transformed in a moment and where writers can affect, provoke and inspire. I want more than a new format. My interest is not so much in fiction as in freedom. I want material with a purpose. I want meaning.

Personally, I need to be inspired but not merely with the cheap thrill of an overplayed drama that only leads people to a spiralling story of hopeless predictability—I need to be truly moved to personal action. I have been sitting in this dungeon of monotony, stifled by the overwhelming fear that the lack of stimulation that has lately driven me to drink has become my life—and quite frankly, I'm dead tired of it.

I skim through to the ending.

> And then one day she would find her own voice.
> Upon her attempt to add lyrics to her performance for the mirror that had been her only stage, she saw her loyal audience and held the lingering eye of her lover. She turned and, staring solidly and directly into his heart, she extended an inviting hand. She opened her soul and, once again, began to hear the sweet music of her flamenco guitar. He knew it was time for his long-awaited lesson. She knew she would again feel free.

As personally resigned to the entire process of manuscript reviewing as I have become over the past few months, after briefly reading through this young writer's proposal, I finally believe there just might be hope for me at the end of this day, and our next author may be as close as a phone call.

I pick up my cell from the desk and call Dane. Excited, I address him before he even has time to answer.

"Barnett?"

"Hey, hon."

"I got it."

"Never had any doubt, sweetheart," he replies without so much as a clue as to what I am talking about.

"Written by a young girl from a small island in Mexico. Isla Mujeres—the Island of Women," I explain, the words spilling out.

"What's the story?"

"Naked dancing gypsy of any interest?" I answer, teasing him.

"Conjures a few images," he responds in his boyish enthusiasm, only one of the many characteristics about him that has kept me as his loyal right hand for many years now.

"All kidding aside, more of a spiritual journey, I think. I'll need to go down and get the full story," I proclaim confidently, feeling secured by his unwavering faith in my ability to produce and, of course, grateful for his patience with the time it sometimes takes for me to get here. Even when I lose sight, Dane always seems to hold on, until I finally discover the one critical beacon that makes all the difference to me in finding my way back home.

"Let's meet first thing," he says. "I want every last detail."

∞∞∞∞∞∞∞∞

I've held a few jobs in life but have spent the majority of my career working directly with Dane Barnett, founder and owner of Barnett Publishing Inc.—BPI—one of the largest privately held publishing firms in North America. With over twenty-two years in existence, the company houses seventy-five different magazine publications in nine different languages with over twenty-five hundred employees worldwide, along with an extensive portfolio of highly acclaimed novels by first-time writers, lately a specialty of ours.

My job involves not only writing magazine articles and independent correspondence, but also attending business and social events as well as reviewing new material, potential clients and any possible innovative business ventures for BPI. Clearly, my role is to find the diamond in the rough, using whatever tool of measurement I deem effective. I tend to rely on only one—intuition, and specifically, my own.

This makes my life a passionate one to say the least. I'm always on the move somewhere, looking for something other than what is directly in front of me. This eternal search creates a dramatic life where movements are profound, and action, compulsive. But as for a life of any intimacy, time tends to limit all exploration and depth, a lifestyle that works very well for me, for the most part.

∞∞∞∞∞∞

Standing now to look over the mecca of tiny bright lights suspended and quietly lounging in the black night air, I see the carefully defined points of interest in the city, and the life that exists in the near distance. I watch and listen. The wind is still, while a low hum from the dwindling day lingers through the open window. I hear people and cars in the background but do not see any. I watch the ocean as it floats quietly in the distance and reaches out and beyond, to what feels like never land, and wonder what it's like, and when I, personally, will get there. Vancouver, I think as I breathe deeply. Many think Dane and I should be based elsewhere, but my only question would be, And why? Why would I want to give up this wide-open horizon for a cubbyhole and a concrete slab at this point? We travel so much as it is that, when I'm home, I want the water at my feet and the mountains within view. I want to open my window and smell the melancholy mix of evergreen forest and damp, mineral-rich earth. I want to be an arm's length from Stanley Park's sweet invitation, and ready and waiting to respond, as often as her fresh Pacific breeze calls.

I smile and turn, leaving the stilled freighters awaiting their docks, and light the large scented candles sitting on their brushed copper stands. Extracting a long thin box of wooden matches from behind the hand-crafted picture frame that rests on the mantle, I glance at the photo of Dane and me from the gala last New Year's Eve. Thank God for that shot—at least there was one memory captured. Champagne just seems to be the death of me. I find its momentary extravagance is always most enjoyable; only the remorseful recollection the following day, if there is any at all, makes my exuberant consumption hard to swallow.

Men and champagne have their similarities.

Dragging this afternoon's manicured toes in long, velvet strokes across my Persian rug, I make my way to the kitchen where a bottle of my favourite Rioja sits and awaits consumption. I pull a large crystal goblet from the top of the wine rack and place it carefully on the granite counter in front of me. I pour myself a generous mid-level glass and recall the afternoon I first discovered this exact selection, in its subterranean cellar in the heart of the Ribera del Duero region, while making my way through northern Spain.

Being forty, never married and successfully employed now for many years, I have definitely benefited from the single life—it has provided me with the freedom to travel on whim and to gain experience without compromise at any given moment. I suppose a partner might supply more at times, and on occasion I did attempt to find one, but there was always the risk—and as the abrupt end of my relationship with Julian clearly proved once again—the futility.

To be successful in any worthwhile venture, whether romantic or otherwise, I find a solid sense of security . . . fundamental, for without it you've got nothing. And from what I have learned, particularly over the past while, the only way to truly guarantee such success, quite frankly, is to manage all matters alone.

Delicately handling my wine, I re-enter the living room and slip into the fat cushion of my buttermilk leather sofa, both pleased and exhausted with my results from today. Flipping the small metal switch under the end table, I shut off the Venetian lamp hanging directly above my head and lean back to relax in the warm scented candlelight, breathing in the hints of simmering vanilla. Finally able to release my mind from work for the moment, I listen to Mozart still playing quietly, thinking how his music is like the hidden and untapped secret to life. Wolfgang knew what it was all about, and you could hear it if you really listened. With small innuendos leading here and there, stanzas of repetition providing lessons over and over and over again, each have their altered accentuation and surprise. Staccato, period, comma, crescendo—all is inevitably tied to the whole. Focus, concentrate, read between the lines; understand the passion, the perfection and the purpose held within the structure. That's what he was saying—it's the structure that matters. Within the structure you can hear, appreciate the lesson, and yet still venture freely within its realm, exploring, all the while continuing to maintain the integrity of the whole. Like a playground where you can still learn without losing, and gain without grovelling, I think as I take a sip of my wine and savour the lust of a now completely expanded grape.

I concentrate on his message. Together his slow motion graduates to pandemonium, all for the production of harmony, finally reaching its desired pursuit of meaning, granting an understanding of its entirety, like a rainbow does at the end of a storm. There is a purpose in each element, a function, a role. Applause, then acknowledgement with the last sweet exhale: release is granted when discovery is sought. Writers are found when readers never give up. Pockets of gold are recovered when the rain is endured. To get there, however, one has to journey, venture, reach, find, fight—and trust. Understanding in the end is secondary, unimportant. Keeping the faith truly matters. Turning the pages makes the difference. Waiting until the rain has fallen, and hearing the symphony played out is what grants real enjoyment. With music, like anything in life, understanding does not grant satisfaction. True fulfillment is only reached in the experience. It's unfortunate that Julian was not able to stick around long enough to discover the difference.

Enough of my own personal saga: I have spent sufficient time there in the past few months, and I will not be edging back now. I have found my writer, and very soon, I will be en route to a small island in Mexico to meet her and finalize our next deal, and that is all that matters to me now.

Lifting my wine to the candle beside me, I watch the light cast its reflection through the refined crystal. Shining with its brilliance, much like the boastful red of the robin's breast, proudly bringing the news of the advent of spring, I watch its glow and realize that I, too, will now have a story to share. I raise a final toast to Mozart's renowned *Requiem*, a composition that would ironically come to honour his own departing and celebrate the release of the things that no longer carry any life for me. Taking another slow sip of tonight's satisfaction, I feel enthusiasm rumble through my body, much like a deep, rolling storm just about to break.

A new season is soon to unfold—I can feel it.

TWO

For me there is only the traveling on paths that have heart, on any path that may have heart. There I travel, and the only worthwhile challenge is to traverse its full length. And there I travel, looking, looking breathlessly.

—Don Juan

I look up from what seems like a large hole in the earth, miles from anything. I am disconnected and alone. The earth around me is wet and damp, but my heart is dry and desolate, like an empty crater in the middle of my body. I see a tiny blue light shining in this massive black sky above me. Despite my lack of energy, its brightness calls me forward. From a distance, the light is clear and distinct, beautiful and focused. Somehow I find a way to break through my overwhelming resignation. Carefully and methodically, I begin to climb.

    Placing my hands on the dark rock, I feel life slowly seep into my fingers as I pull myself up from the bottom. The blue light grows larger as the black slowly retreats until it is only an outline around the deep blue centre. My accomplishment is slow and calculated, but encouraging. I struggle and continue until only the blue light remains. I enter a magical land that is deep and rich and abundant. I take my final step and climb to the surface. I have made it, or so it seems. Then, in that very moment, the vision fades. I step back, and all is black.

∞∞∞∞∞∞∞∞

An indigo light revealing that it's 5:37 a.m. beams brightly from the alarm clock on my nightstand. With my eyes wide open, I lie still with the back of my hand resting across my forehead, staring at the start to my day and scouring the attic of my mind for insight.

My dream is back, drifting in as unpredictably as the passing events in my life, frequently inspirational, but more often without any clarity at all. The visual itself is always vivid and in colour. The meaning behind it, however, is not as distinct and often leaves me to wake wondering and confused. Each episode follows a sequence that always begins the same and periodically alters slightly in its ending. I wonder what the message is this time.

∞∞∞∞∞∞∞∞

As scheduled, Dane and I meet at 7:30 a.m. sharp.

"OK, so what have we got here, Nate?" he eagerly questions as soon as we sit down together in the boardroom.

"Jasmine Dubois. Unpublished true story of a woman's spiritual journey," I report as I open the proposal and take a long, slow sip of my coffee.

"And where'd you say she was?"

"Isla Mujeres—the Island of Women."

"What do you know about it?" Dane asks as he swirls his charcoal leather captain's chair to one side and leans back in contemplation, one hand lying flat on the table beside him.

"Believed to be ruled by Ixchel, the goddess of women and fertility, according to the Mayan mythology. She's famous for her duality—grants childbirth and abundance, but also uses destructive storms to cleanse the earth for rebirth and renewal. In ancient times women came from all over to worship her," I answer and think about a clean slate for myself. I have no idea what this would even look like but know that if there were such a goddess out there and she granted new beginnings, I would find her and get one.

"The story–follows the mandate we want?" Dane continues.

"From everything I've seen."

"You think it's a go?"

"Yeah, I do," I reply.

∞∞∞∞∞∞∞∞

I had no proof other than the print in front of me, but the familiar nudge that taps at the very core of my being told me that an essential factor was missing from this story, the finding of which, I knew, was going to expand my mind into an entirely new realm and beyond. Whether I had an audience at that moment or not, I knew I could not ignore the lead this time. Call it an instinct, or even just a hunch, but something screamed that my life depended on it. Something told me if I didn't take this step right here and now, I was going to lose everything I had accomplished thus far. If I could have known how profoundly my entire reality would shift, and how much my life would indeed alter, I am unsure that I would ever have had the courage to move forward in this moment. Fortunately, however, there is an unforeseen magic about life that conceals certain paths and hides the unknown and inevitable truth, blindly guiding us until we are ready for its full acceptance.

∞∞∞∞∞∞∞∞

"Let's set it up today," Dane announces, lightly tapping the top of the table and moving his hand along the side to cradle its rounded ledge.

"You all right if I head down for a few weeks, then?" I ask, already knowing his answer.

"Absolutely. Let's arrange it within the next couple," he says before leaning forward to question me directly, deep in his all-serious and intimate inquiry.

"Are you sure you're up for this, Nate? I know all this stuff with Julian . . ."

"Are you kidding me? Timing's the best part," I respond quickly, firmly ending any further question around my own current emotional well-being and knowing without a doubt if there ever were a time for leaving, now is definitely that time.

Once we finish with all pressing preliminaries, I head back to my office to skim over the Dubois proposal one last time before making the call. Whether it's the intrigue of the Mayan mystic, or the fact that I will be in the heart of the Mexican Caribbean in just a few days, I feel relieved and ready. Vacating my tight little two-bit world of instant and incessant romantic reminders is just what I need right now, and hopefully the distance will sever the lingering cobwebs of stale emotion left over from Julian that still seem to be relentlessly weaving their way into my head each night.

It'll be three years Friday since the night we first met, the night of his gallery opening. So much has happened since then, I think, as I slip back and reminisce about an entirely different life, now more as observer rather than participant. I reflect on the scenes of the past 1,095 days like a movie I have watched many times before; I am familiar with all events and can regurgitate each and every line with only the slightest cue, but my emotions now seem once removed and somewhat foreign.

∞∞∞∞∞∞∞

Dane had insisted I meet him for cocktails at seven that evening; he wanted to introduce me to his friend, "the Painter," which smelled like two things to me: an all-too-smooth dinner date and a two-week affair that would end with the promise, "I'll call you in a bit," and I'd never hear from the man again. Dane's request, however, was that I trust him. Never trust anything that doesn't grow—that was my motto. An old wives' tale I picked up from an ancient gardening manual at my grandmother's place as a child, but my grandmother was a wise woman and, even at a young age, I knew she had things lying around for a reason. I kept that one small, ancient clipping nailed to my brain like a treasured roadmap, continually using its simple wisdom as my only valued and trustworthy bullshit barometer.

At 6:45 p.m., despite my severe aversion to the cat-and-mouse semantics of meeting a friend of a friend, I did find myself looking for a red crumbled-brick warehouse and a parking space in the industrial section of town tucked under the bridge near the bay.

Now, the secret in following any path of intuition is listening. The effort and the patience this can take can often impede success, but questions do surface for a reason. And how useful was this information to me the night I met Julian? About as handy as a leash is for a pet that has already left home—a perfectly effective safeguard when put to use in a timely manner. I, however, was like your beloved Fifi. Despite knowing all the beneficial and protective properties of such a proven practice, I had already mindlessly strayed at the first scent of distraction.

∞∞∞∞∞∞∞∞

As I reach the building, the image of a small, young child entering a huge, old castle flashes through my mind like a daunting, dark scene from *Jack and the Beanstalk*. I get a sense of cold corridors and large empty spaces and other tormented tales, like the princess trapped in the tower, sentenced to a life she does not want and forever searching with no way out. With all the makings of a fairy tale gone wrong, I still continue to pull the heavy iron ring in the middle of the door and enter, despite the terribly weighted feeling of giants and secrets and old hiding places. Ignoring the more intelligent and much younger side of myself, I blindly step forward into a foreign kingdom and into the life of a man about whom I know absolutely nothing.

Dane spots me immediately as I enter the foyer and waves me over. I make my way through the crowd to the bar to join him and, of course, his friend whom, if observation serves me, he now has polished, propped and waiting.

"Natalie Lauren, 'the Painter.'" He introduces us calmly, but with the excitement of a giddy school boy a quarter of his age. He so thought he had this one in the bag.

"Painter," I oblige with the playful sass I am well-known to bring to such an occasion and extend both my well-versed performance and my hand toward Julian.

"Julian Miras. Very nice to meet you, Natalie," he says, reaching out and elegantly reciprocating my gesture in his gallantly warm and well-groomed manner.

The Painter is sexy, extremely, in all honesty. His hair, tied back, is dark and striking, yet soft with a natural highlight. His face is ridged with clear definition; he has a strong jawline, smooth unblemished skin and a well-manicured goatee—cut short—which frames his perfectly sculptured lips. His eyes are piercingly dark, almost deadly, while his glance is sensual but not intrusive. A blatant contrast exists in his appearance. The play of expression across his face ranges from intent to tranquil, much like a warrior who lives the life of a prince. I wonder if this is by design or default. Seeing the possibility of both saint and sinner, I question if anyone ever really holds a true balance. The small voice in my head whispers a cynical checklist, analyzing as if supreme judge to a universal contest of authenticity. I scan for the hidden, knowing nothing is simple.

"Cocktail, Ms. Lauren?" Julian offers shortly after our introduction.

"Absolutely," I respond, still remaining in character.

"Christian." Julian gestures as he directs the bartender's attention toward us and wipes his hand smoothly over the stainless steel counter in front of me.

Watching his sensual and mindful movement, I feel a funnel of warm energy clear down to my tailbone, as if he has just draped his hand over my entire bare spine. If this is his first attempt at flirtation, it has worked. Distracted by the hair now standing on the back of my neck and realizing that the arrogant actor I brought into the room has now been dismissed, I struggle to remain present. Julian's voice seems to act as a homing device, however, and helps redirect my mind back to the moment as he continues with his introduction.

"Natalie Lauren. Natalie works with Dane at BPI."

Christian smiles, wipes his black silk tie down the front of his chest, pulling my attention to its design. As he reaches across the bar to shake my hand, I note that his tie has only a few small white flecks in a sea of black silk. As I shake his hand, I wonder if his chosen fashion wear is in any way representative of his character.

He is hospitable and slick. Good characteristics for a man in his position, I presume. I am not convinced I would trust him with any honesty. He appears to be a man who always gets exactly what he wants and someone who never falls shy of the appropriate words to guarantee it. He is a positioner. I am suspicious of anyone named Christian. Judgmental I may be, but more often than not, I usually do find at least a slim ribbon of truth in my first impressions.

"Welcome, Ms. Lauren." His voice is charming and contrived, as I expect. "May I offer you a drink?" he asks slyly as he tilts his head, seemingly accommodating, but analyzing my every move.

Positioners are distinguished by their need for information, and they usually extract it with ease by posing in polite service to their subjects, who, in turn, volunteer all the details they require, without even conscious knowledge. In the game of positioning, a successful player needs to plan and place, and is required to know, understand and accommodate every action and reaction before actually aligning position and gaining control. I am aware of the game, and I know Mr. Christian is definitely an active participant.

"Sapphire martini, rocks . . . twist?" Julian interjects, obviously knowing my answer.

"Couldn't help myself," Dane admits to me quietly under his breath.

"No. I'm sure it was tough," I sarcastically tease, wondering what other fine details Cupid has so helplessly exchanged while the two of them have been awaiting my arrival.

"Bombay, rocks, twist," Christian announces as he hands me my drink.

"Thank you," I acknowledge and accept the cocktail.

Smiling with a guarded collectedness, I glance directly at Julian as Dane toasts to the success of the evening. And, of course, knowing Dane to the extent that I do, I know he is not simply referring to the gallery opening. Lifting the cold crystal rock glass to my mouth, I take a sip of the chilled gin and stare forward as the familiar hint of fresh lemon serves to calmly trickle down the back of my throat, leaving me cooled and secure for the moment. I stand silently, pleased with the secrets.

After several minutes of surprisingly relaxed exchange, Julian politely excuses himself and attends to his other guests, while Dane and I make our way through the sparsely decorated room of aged brick and wrought-iron design to view the paintings. The gallery itself is open and inviting, perfect to expand those less-talented, non-artistic types who tend to think within restricted frameworks. The walls curve to define the area's boundary. Lumpy and concrete, they are painted white and disguise any underlying imperfection. The manipulation of the decor seems odd to me as I make my way about the room. It is the artist's job to unveil this rawness, is it not?

I watch Julian as he gracefully mingles with an intense look of concentration, sincerely acknowledging his potential clients yet never becoming fixated on any particular guest. He is a professional. His movements are both open and ambiguous as he evolves from one role to the next. Again, I am uncertain whether this is by choice or by chance. I have yet to decipher if this is an unconcealed ability or a secretive agenda for this unknown warrior, but my every bone assures me there is definitely something yet to be revealed. Oddly, this ambiguity is not reflected in his work at all.

Julian's paintings inspire this universal connectedness and have a depth to them I have never seen before. With his combinations of rich colours and complex textures, he magically creates these individual worlds of precise clarity and stillness, leaving you not only feeling peaceful, but also centred and open for a much grander inquiry, making the entire experience mystical, intense and fulfilling.

Personally, I find myself drawn into this discovery, to the exploration of the unknown, and am amazed at how I can simply stand to look at an object hanging on a wall in front of me and be provoked to such an internal investigation of what I might find inspiring. Physically, I do not move, but I feel this longing to embrace the passion and freedom of reckless adventure, all the while standing still and feeling safe, whole and complete. I almost want to say his work is medicinal in some way, but it's not. Medicinal, to me, often implies temporary relief, but there is no space for escape here at all. His paintings are rooted and real and have within them this intense commitment that draws you in and holds you there, almost as if they were nurturing you.

In fact, I realize, they are nurturing me, filling me in the same way nature does. I feel the warm night breeze move in, carrying with it the smell of damp cedar, and I hear the wind gently rock the branches overhead, bringing the layers of their small, crisp leaves together. Although I am in a room of concrete and canvas, the world around me feels incredibly alive and connected.

"How did you and Julian meet?" I question Dane, as we stand and watch him from across the room. He is talking to a tall man who looks like he has just returned from a long, hot vacation—he is tanned, with silver hair, and sports a chain with a small turquoise stone medallion around his wrist.

"Friend in New York—Marty. Guy I went to NYU with. Made plans to meet for lunch while I was in town. Had a couple of meetings, wanted me to tag along."

"Marty . . . He's in real estate, isn't he?"

"Yep. Big ticket, heavy hitter. Colleague of his was developing some property for a group of artists. Had a meeting that afternoon, and Julian was there."

"Hmmm," I mouth in contemplation and attempt to piece together the details involved in such a meeting and what Julian's role may have possibly been in it.

"Hmmm," Dane mimics with pronounced and probing emphasis. "Do I detect a hint of intrigue, Lauren? Little entice, little flavour?" he teases.

"Interesting, Barnett. Merely interesting," I admit, pulling up my guard once again and leaving alone any further inquiries about Julian for the evening.

∞∞∞∞∞∞

The morning following my seemingly harmless introduction to the Painter, I am scheduled to fly to the Bahamas and, although definitely not unimpressed with my new acquaintance, I feel that my focus would be better trained on work at the moment than on the potential of any new budding romance. Thus I leave my thoughts of the talented Julian Miras for another time.

Dane offered to charter me directly, but I have decided to catch American Airlines flight 7082 at 9:00 a.m. to L.A. and then on to Miami from there. I am ambivalent in this regard. On the one hand, I am a business executive who expects only the finest of accommodation—nothing short of five-star excellence—while, on the other, I am a young girl constantly craving a simple existence and anonymity. I want all the fineries in the life of a princess and, yet, endlessly search for a quiet, humble man who lives in a trailer park. Sometimes, it's the last dollar spent on a cheap bottle of wine that can make all the difference, I lightly joke to myself, knowing all too well from where my uncertainty stems.

This ambiguity, I believe, originates from a long history of watching my mother battle with the powerful imbalances of her own mind, ranging dangerously between frenzied euphoria and sluggish depression. Her continuous bouts of theatrical psychosis left paths of unusually clear and incredibly creative moments, where madness eventually and inevitably lead to irritable despair and the wretched need to be secluded. My excitement came from watching these emotions dance for her, knowing she created the entire scenario. In my mind a string of incidents still lingers and reminds me of my mother's unique outlook on life. With her, you never knew what you were going to learn each day.

I look out over the large, white floating clouds and beyond to the pale blue horizon as I drop back into earlier years and my childhood.

∞∞∞∞∞∞∞∞

We had driven down the coast as a family and stopped for a picnic outside a small cottage near the water's edge, parallel to the beach. My mother brought a plastic, quilted tablecloth splashed with abstract designs of big, bright red and purple sunflowers. My father, Samuel, sat facing the ocean with his chair twisted to one side, enthralled with reading his *National* and his ever-consuming numbers. My mother chipped away at him, despite his aloofness, in her all-inclusive and flamboyant performance.

"Yellow sunflowers. Oh, for God's sake, why? Why would anyone ever want yellow sunflowers?" she piped, flailing her arms dramatically while arranging our table. She did not see anything within the lines. "Rules—they're unnatural, unproductive," she schooled us in a theatrical, deep Southern accent. "People are born to live, to explore, to discover."

I watched her pink, flowered skirt flounce around the end of the table as she straightened the plastic cloth across its surface and smiled to herself. She was a smart woman. As subservient as her actions tended to be, she knew her voice alone commanded the reality of our family and that her moods moulded our entire future. Anything was possible for her.

"My mother told me, and I never listened. You've gotta make your own way, Nattie. Never let anyone draw your line," she continued, posing with her hands on her hips, facing both my younger brother, Brendan, and me.

"Rules are for needlework, not nations. Right, Sammie?" she said as she winked at me and flittingly jerked to lightly tweak the top of my father's head with a kiss.

"Mmm-hmm," my father agreeably hummed, looking up from his paper and slightly over the edge of his reading glasses, having absolutely no idea what she had just said.

"What do ya call that, Mama? Somethin' that don't need rules?" Brendan asked. He always did like to put a title to things.

"We'll call that 'the Sunflower Theory,'" she answered with slow and exaggerated inflection, still cooing in her rehearsed and thick Southern drawl.

"Why's it called 'the Sunflower Theory,' Mama?" Brendan questioned further.

"Because they both make you smile," my mother said as she smirked at her own brilliance. "Come on, kids, come help your mama. We got food to eat."

∞∞∞∞∞∞∞∞

"Chicken or pasta?" I distantly hear the flight attendant addressing me as the man sitting next to me lightly touches my forearm.

"Chicken, please. Thank you," I acknowledge as she places my meal on the tray in front of me and smiles.

Looking again to the clouds outside of the window, I take a bite of my inflight answer to tonight's dinner and drift again to thoughts of my mother and the Sunflower Theory. She was a powerful woman, my mother. She dealt with the overwhelming weight of never being happy and disposing of all her girlhood dreams and, yet, she kept our home light and cheerful despite the deepest depression that possessed her. As much as she drowned in her personal selfhood, she left us with the impression that each moment in life was a special time to be celebrated. Regardless of where her emotions came from, with a child's instinct for truth I observed feelings that were alive and real.

Passion, I realize now, often equated with hysteria, but those uncontrollable, undefined drastic opposites of frantic emotion granted my mother freedom. The drama made her feel intense and extreme. She was an artist. Not once had I felt this mania to be a form of dysfunction. She was able to go beyond what I saw and so many others denied.

To possess such ability to connect with emotion was rare and special. She was gifted.

As a child, I was, unfortunately, not able to see her obsession with agony. I only saw her feel, and I created guidelines for myself to chart what it would take to feel passion, to feel free. Great emotion was thus only awarded through tremendous struggle for me. Nothing was easy. And drama is what gave life depth.

My mother was a deep woman. She kept the story of life lost so buried within her that we never knew her flirtatious smile belied the chasm that was her soul. I am not sure anyone ever knew the truth.

I smile at the attendant as she extends her hospitable grin and makes her final sweep through the cabin, in preparation for landing. Like my mother, I have many secrets of my own, and I have yet to deal with the fact that the two people I loved most in this world are dead.

"Welcome to balmy Miami, folks. Current temperature is sitting at 24 degrees. Local time, 10:30 p.m.," the pilot announces and continues to inform passengers of gate numbers and connecting flights.

I do not leave now until morning. I head directly to the hotel, excited to jump into a hot shower and drain all the remaining details from my day and, God knows, I am in need of a nightcap.

∞∞∞∞∞∞∞

Feeling refreshed and somewhat relaxed, I throw my wet towel across the armchair near the bed and snuggle my naked body under the crisp sheets that are slightly cool and smell of fresh citrus. Grabbing my drink and the remote control from the night table, I take a long, slow swallow and flip on the television. God, it is one thing for which I no longer have the time. Observing for a few quick moments, I am instantly reminded why—with more than two hundred channels—there is still nothing to watch. How is that even possible? Surveying the senseless images that flicker before my faraway eyes, I eventually decide on a nature show and settle in to learn the deadly and constrictive behaviours of the boa, once again reminded of stifling relationships and the taste of dead partners.

I think back to my recent introduction to Julian at the art gallery and wonder if something beyond all former history might be possible. Even the thought of beginning again is overwhelming and, in all honesty, exhausting.

My heart beats through the cotton sheet as I lie still. Placing my hand flat on my chest, I feel the small drum tap lightly in the centre of my palm. Moments like this are rare, but I do stop and listen. I think of the many generations that have preceded this one, and how the drum once served as such a resourceful instrument of creation for people, beckoning individual or group desires into existence. *You want rain . . . drum, dance, believe, drum . . . you have rain.*

The formula was simple, and the faith—consuming.

As I lie now and feel the slow, repetitive beat against my own skin, I wonder how and why, as a society, we ever strayed so far from something that worked so well and, specifically, when did I? At what point did I stop believing?

As I lie and question, my cell rings on the nightstand.

"What are you wearing?" Dane whispers on the other end of the phone.

"A leather boa," I respond, glancing back at the large, coiling snakes on the full screen.

"Seriously?"

"No, but I am watching a nature show on constrictors," I offer and smirk to myself.

"Nate, you really gotta work on your sexy talk. Honestly, you're so damn literal."

"I will have you know, literal happens to work in my world and certainly has a lot more venues for expression than sexy talk," I defend.

"You never know what you don't try," he chants.

"I'll keep that in mind. What's up?" I ask as I lean back and rub my eyes.

"Just checking in."

"All's well," I report.

"You ever wonder how we end up where we are?" Dane inquires, changing the subject.

"What do you mean?" I respond, knowing full well to what he is referring.

"I started out so strong and determined with a heart that would bang with excitement and idealism, where anything was possible. And, yet, my life is consumed with working hard to maintain an even level. Trying to keep it all together, holding everyone and everything in place, never touching, and actually entirely ignoring, any real truth for myself. Do you ever get like that?"

"Every waking moment, darlin'," I confess.

∞∞∞∞∞∞∞∞

The truth was, I had lost faith. I'd become comfortable in a mediocre life, content in a world I never would have formerly accepted for myself. This is who I had become.

I often tried to convince myself otherwise, but the truth was I'd been living my life from this point of survival for decades—afraid to live, afraid to die, afraid to feel, afraid to be consumed and absolutely refusing to admit any of these fears, for fear of being weak or, God forbid, wrong.

I had so much to do and was scared to death I would die without ever figuring it all out. This silent self-induced suffocation owned me like a slave and dictated my every move and, at times, had me waking in the middle of the night gasping for air, begging for just one more moment to make it all real. But even when these earth-shaking moments came up, I didn't grab the opportunity. I noticed the panic. I felt the desperation. But then I simply let the moment pass and did nothing, except train myself to tolerate more and learn to breathe with less.

∞∞∞∞∞∞∞∞

"Really . . . every moment?" Dane continues.

"Yep, like a cheap carnival game, Barnett."

"What do ya mean?

"Seems like I'm just caught slamming random mole heads as fast as they can arise and thinking I'm somehow winning the game," I reply. "Not realizing my area of coverage has become too big and my foam mallet far too small."

"God, you're brilliant, Lauren," Dane declares.

Like Dane, I have created a solid facade of strength and determination to ensure life looks perfect and well, and I have spent most of my life swimming in this unwavering denial, functioning as a machine, automatically acting and reacting to whatever comes up next and wondering why miracles never seem to happen.

I, too, wonder what it would eventually take. When would I breathe in that one unbearable moment and finally throw in my measly little mallet and pick a new game?

Dane and I discuss our plans for the next couple of days and say good night. In a hotel room that contains nothing of any significance to me, and one I can safely walk away from in the morning without any further accountability or intimate reminder, I allow myself to feel, to touch that lost world of uncertainty, if only briefly. I know I need to decide what is important . . . what I need to be happy . . . what my self needs to be content . . . and, most importantly, what I need to be myself. And I know if I don't, eventually I will sabotage my entire world and everyone in it.

I need to go back and find my unique beat once again. I know I can create something new. I just haven't been able to grant myself that one simple permission to listen to the call of the wild. I don't feel right or wrong in this, only vacant and on hold and like I have been standing here for most of my life.

I take another sip of my cocktail and again let my thoughts slink away. Logic once again clenches its strong fist over my mind, and I convince myself this complacency was not created in one day and certainly is not going to be resurrected tonight. I take a slow, even breath and reassure myself I'd find some time, later. Lying to myself so easily, I once again extend another empty promise I know I will not fulfill and provide myself with a little more time until my conscience again resurfaces. I turn to my left side and let my much-ignored right-brain, heartfelt longings drop back into the reserved and far left corners of my mind, to which they are highly accustomed and where they are comfortably understood.

∞∞∞∞∞∞∞∞∞∞

My wake-up call comes early the next morning. I repack the few things I have taken from my carry-on and make my way to the cab outside.

At the airport, I watch people panicking to secure their first cup of coffee, parents providing their children with a vending machine's most nutritional alternative to breakfast and others deciphering their next travel arrangement. I detect habits and tolerance, home life and hassles. Noting the varying degrees of love and respect found in the assorted combinations, I piece together a personal checklist of what I, myself, would want from a partner. You never know when it will come in handy. We board.

At 10:30 a.m. local time I finally arrive. I throw my bag over my shoulder, grab the rest of my luggage and hail a cab. My place is on the opposite side of the island, and although I will need to return to the central core in the next couple of days, I am off to the villa and then to the beach.

By early afternoon I am finally alone at the ocean, waves washing my perfectly manicured toes, and nothing to do but rub the gentle and repetitive wetness into my skin.

Bending, I rest my heels at the water's edge and play with the sand at my feet. Staring out at the bright, open horizon, I feel as free as a young child sent to play without adult supervision.

To my immediate right, I notice two sad, long eyes staring at me through a large piece of saturated driftwood. Moving my cheek slightly, I see a hot and very pregnant dog resting under what little shade is available. Although never pregnant myself, I can relate to her desperate need for quiet space. We sit.

Gazing at this panting mother-to-be, I watch her swollen stomach expand for extended gasps and sympathize with her limitation. She looks foreign, abnormal in her own body and, yet, completely natural. Again, I relate. Often feeling like a guest in my own life, where many watch and assume I naturally belong in it, I never feel completely at home and I'm constantly praying for any way out.

How *did* we ever end up here, I question, as I stare at the large maternal mound that now houses her next playful litter and attempt to telepathically continue last night's conversation with my new friend, whom I have decided to call Max. Max is a fit name, an autograph of a character and a personality that could stand on its own. Always thought it would be a great name for a child, if I ever had one.

Max rests her drooping lids to feel the single breeze offered in the hot afternoon sun, and I, too, close my eyes and allow nature to cool my own swelling from the thick and unaccustomed humidity. We sit quietly, a comfortable distance from each other for hours, with no need to reach or coddle or fix anything about each other. We simply sit and allow each to be. Parallel, with one foot extended into the water, and the other underneath our respective bodies in the sand, we rest. Despite the individual histories that may have got us this far, Max and I are able to lounge lazily and allow each to be, not for any particular reason, but just because we can exist as we are, content and understood.

I smile in adoration of life's simple lessons, of pregnant dogs and of quiet afternoons by the ocean.

THREE

Holding on to anger is like grasping a hot coal with the intent of throwing it at someone else; you are the one getting burned.

—Buddha

"Just follow that road till you get to a green sign that says Coral Road. Turn left, all the way to the end. There's a spot there, Honey Comb. Go in, ask for Sugar. Tell him Adelaide sent ya. He'll look after ya," the woman at the beach house explains two days later as she stands and holds her antique bicycle steady for me.

I climb on.

"That's all I need to know?" I question her again, knowing I can manage a deal without even the blink of an eye in any given moment, delegating and directing without so much as taking a breath; but when it comes to the basic four cardinals of any physical arena, I am simply a disoriented and moronic mess.

People tell me it's innate, that you're born with it. I can tell you for certain that a sense of direction is one quality not sown in this Nate. I have no internal compass whatsoever. And the thing is, I never know I'm truly lost until I'm there and have to confess my situation to some random stranger walking by, which in itself takes everything I've got at the time. And even then, as far as I can see, the only benefit this acknowledgement offers is to drench me in further panic, making me feel as if I will never find my way back.

"That's all you need. Simple as coconut pie."

"All right," I skeptically reply, thank Adelaide and start on my way, thinking that in my world coconut pie is the last thing from simple, sweetheart.

A positive attitude, I realize, however, is essential. Forced optimism is the only useful tool I have found in combating my chronic disorientation. Always start with a positive attitude, I tell myself, because there's a very good chance you're either going to need it or lose it along the way. If there is one thing I have learned, and rather roughly, I might add, it is this: It does not in any way serve your purpose or overall goal to scream at those trying to help you find your destination. As frustrated as you are or may become at another's utter stupidity, it is best to keep this opinion to yourself at all times and simply look for a different answer. Screaming, you will find, at a stupid person does not make him or her smarter and shouting at someone who cannot even hear what you are saying, or is merely choosing not to listen, in the end actually makes you, and only you, the raging idiot. Hindsight, more often than not, will prove, in essence, that your stupidity got you lost in the first place, and the person whom you are now soliciting for direction couldn't care less if you ever found your way home. So, blaming another for his or her lack of communication skills, although seemingly highly justified at any particular moment, will not get you there any quicker and, depending on the person directing you, may just get you right back to where you started. Trust me.

"Best ceviche on the island," Adelaide calls after me as I ride off.

I wave my hand in acknowledgement and begin, pedalling to the repetitive squeak of the ancient beach cruiser she has lent me. Calmed and trusting, I set off on my journey through the countryside and head in the direction Adelaide has so kindly laid out.

A sultry breeze lifts my hair lightly over my shoulders, like a once-ravished and now-forgotten lover, leaving me with a lingering flash of intense seduction from its familiar and suggestive nudge. I blink slowly and savour the sensuality of the moment, enjoying each memory while it lasts as I weave down the road and make my way to the nearby local village. The slightly rolling hillside waves into a rich span of fat, green lushness and holds no boundaries. My path is open, wild and free. My mind accommodates as much as possible.

Once at the sea-green sign, I turn left, as instructed, and coast down into the village with precision and a secret sense of accomplishment, now reassured that I am on the right path. People stand along the roadside and watch as I ride by. Venturing past crumbled buildings and open doorways, I finally arrive at the restaurant, happy with myself that I have found the right place without a major episode. The washed-out, yellow-painted front door squeaks as I enter and walk in to address the man standing behind the bar.

"Hi, I'm looking for Sugar."

"Everybody lookin' for Sugar. Don't I look like Sugar? Brown Sugar. Yes, not just your normal sugar sweetness, but the good, natural, dark and unrefined cane. Muscovado." The tall, lean man moves slowly with a slight athletic strut and laughs to himself.

"I'm Sugar, honey," he responds as he turns toward me.

The smell of last night's spilled gin wafts from the bar and is very similar to the tainted breeze that drifts directly from the mouth of its owner as he faces me.

"Hi, I'm Natalie," I say, introducing myself. "Adelaide sent me. Thought I might like your ceviche."

"Oh now, she did, did she? Ms. Addy . . ." He quietly reflects as if there may have been a charmed history between the two of them at one point or another and then continues.

"Well, we don't get much complaint," he says slowly.

"And those who do, we just throw 'em in the ocean, let 'em get their own damn fish." He smirks at me and winks.

"Well . . . good. Good," I repeat, somewhat distracted, yet still with a polite and horizontal lip.

I take a deep breath and look around the quaint little joint, gathering a quick sense of the place. The room is stark and quite small with no furniture except for a couple of men leaning against the side wall, who look like they may very well be permanent fixtures about the place.

"Well, let's get ya started, Ms. Natalie," he says as he opens the rust-speckled cooler behind him and pulls out a large glass jar of juice and pours me a brimming plastic cupful.

"Can't start your mornin' wid out a li'l fresh juice," he says as he wipes down the counter in front of me and hands me my cup.

"On da house. Any guest of Ms. Addy's is a guest of mine." He smiles as he leans forward with his hands folded together and taps the bar surface with the heels of his palms.

"Thank you." I accept the cup as I watch Sugar pour another big cup for himself.

"Lotsa tables outside. Bedda git da one ya want. She fills quick," he informs me. "Not only da tourists come ta see da Sugar," he teases as he takes a large drink of his juice and turns back to arranging his bar.

I make my way outside as Sugar has suggested and select a large wooden spool which has once been used to coil cable telephone wire and now functions as Honey Comb's fine decor. Choosing a seat still in the shade and close to the water, I lean back and relax under the palm tree. There is nothing much here except for a handful of spools and some old wooden chairs scattered around them. Placing my plastic cup on the table's weathered surface, I rest my feet on its peeled painted base and wonder what the hell little Ms. Addy has got me into. As I sit back, however, I notice that I do feel relaxed and, for a moment, have no concerns at all.

Staring out at the crystal water, I can feel its blanket of heat from here as I watch a single rowboat bob with the wave's rhythm, lazily moving up and down, never fighting its natural flow. I have never been as obedient, I think, as I take a sip of my fresh coconut juice, soon to discover it contains one serious and seductive slip of island gin—I take another small swig to confirm. No, I have never been as obedient. As I chew the distinctive bittersweet layers of shredded pulp, I respectfully watch the owner, proud and hospitable, entertaining his friends as they gather to fill his restaurant; I realize that in some ways old Sugar is much richer than I will ever be.

The day's catch soon arrives. Two heavy-set men with tight white T-shirts and impressive arms empty their large sacks of shellfish on a long, thin table that directly faces the crowd, now increasing in size. Sugar begins to prepare our feast. Like any restaurateur, he has his own style whereby his years of practice make his job seem effortless and masterful. One hand wields the machete and slices wedges of lemons, limes and oranges, while the other squeezes ripe citrus over the freshly sliced conch as he prepares each bowl individually. One by one, we eventually all indulge in a humble man's honest day and follow with his traditional thirst-quenching juice, while a few in the crowd alternate with their recent fish stories and their latest jackpot on playing the numbers. I sit and listen, not feeling the slightest need to be anywhere else other than right here, at this moment.

"Ever been to Baha's?" a local man named Thomas asks much later in the day.

"No," I respond, hearing its name for the first time.

"New restaurant around here and, let me tell ya, food's the bomb," he says as he winks at me, clicks his tongue to the side of his cheek and gestures a big thumbs up, reminding me of a used-car salesman trying to meet quota. He is clearly someone who has been enjoying his gin and juice this afternoon.

The others are in agreement, however, and a group of us all decide to head for dinner across the bay. I am to meet Eman, our associate, a bit later tonight and decide to call him to see if he wants to come and join us.

"Hello," he answers calmly with his signature rich and majestic charm, a feature that has always led me to believe he is a direct descendant of real nobility and someone who not only holds the respect of the gods, but also possesses this great heavenly power to summon all magical goodness with only the sound of his voice.

"Hello, Eman," I tease with a counteractive and gin-induced rhythm.

"Natalie, how are you?" he gently questions. "Dane said you arrived two days ago."

"There's a group of us going for dinner across the bay. Wanna come meet me?"

"Where are you?"

"On the other side."

"Of course you are." He laughs lightly.

We have been close friends for many years now, and Eman is well-acquainted with my voracious appetite for new cultural adventures and my never-ending demand to be slightly off the grid and continually on the move.

"We're heading to Baha's. Do you know it?"

"Intimately."

"Really?" I smile, intrigued, but not overly shocked at his response. Eman is a brilliant investor with a solid mind for great business and as much as we talk, he always does seem to have a pending surprise or two waiting quietly on the horizon.

"I own it," he reveals.

"Perfect. We won't need to worry about directions."

"I'll call ahead. We'll see ya around seven, love."

Sugar offers to store Addy's bicycle in the back of the restaurant for me and has promised to personally return it a little later in the evening, which I'm convinced is only going to sprinkle a little extra sweetness on both of their days. Marco assists me. Marco is forty-six, tall, very fit, and tanned; with his fair hair and ice-blue eyes, he is quite attractive, but his lightness ends there. There is a weight to Marco that prevents him from seeing the silver lining of any cloud. Literally, he ages you as he speaks. I am clear now he has only offered to help me because I am the freshest ear to his old story and, once again, I am reminded of the adage, favours are *never* free. With the less-than-concentrated effort one tends to have after an afternoon of relaxed consumption at the water's edge, we finally saunter through the sand and along the beach in the direction of the water taxis.

A developer originally from London, Marco has lived on the island for approximately nine years and has talked incessantly all afternoon about his construction plans. Although quite successful while in London, he is frustrated with his life here, informing me of the various zoning restrictions that often impede his desired progress and those that continually act as his greatest obstacles.

I lend half an ear to his ranting and wonder about the possibility of Dane and I bypassing all the political entanglement he is talking about. At the same time, however, I question the legitimacy of his issues and what it is that he is really saying. There's a way they do business down here. There is a way the entire world does business. I have no interest in playing the victim. I have spent sufficient time in tragedy and, quite frankly, I am bored with its limited realm. I am sick of weak excuses and pathetic people. He is adamant about these restrictions, however, and continues to express his argument repeatedly, wrongly assuming I am someone who actually gives a damn about the situation at this point. There is only one way of accomplishment for people like Marco and, from his stories, it appears not to be working and he just can't seem to grasp the concept.

 Farther down along the beach, a large fishing boat pulls in and slowly docks. A group of six men quietly file onto shore, shaking hands with each other as they separate. Although appropriately dressed for the hot climate, a local fishing tour does not look like it has been on their agenda. Seeing their boat suspiciously empty of any gear, equipment or fish, I predict I am correct in my assumptions. As I watch the very affluent looking group, their subtle and calculated movements tell me they are about money and are led, controlled and consumed by its insatiable accumulation. They are certainly not here for fish-fries and rum cocktails.

 More substantially evident, however, aside from their dock of entry, are the vehicles waiting for them at the road. On this side of the island, cars are reserved for only those of privileged position and the ones that await them far surpass any transportation of a prestigious local. I scan the crowd, seeing only the backs of their finely pressed linen shirts, for the most part. The man directing the group, and the last to leave the boat, looks slightly over his left shoulder before they disembark. Although I can only catch a small glimpse from here, I swear it is the same man I saw the other night at Julian's opening. As he reaches to cordially pat the right shoulder of his colleague, I see a bright flash on his wrist from the reflection of something metal in the sun. Although clear focus is not entirely possible from where I am currently standing, I am certain that quick, glimmering streak comes from a silver chain with a turquoise stone medallion. As I look again, I am now convinced that he not only holds a close and haunting resemblance to the strange man I saw talking to Julian at the art gallery the other night, but he is, in fact, the same one.

"Ms. Natalie, ya gonna miss da bo'." The group beckons as I quickly grab a strong hand and jump aboard.

My mind races, questioning the likelihood of being halfway across the continent and seeing someone I have been in a room with a few days ago on the West Coast. I readjust the knot in the front of my blouse and place my small leather shoulder bag on the floor at my feet. We head in the direction of the island.

Once we are on the other side, a taxi drives us along the southern tip, right along the beach. Marco continues his history of the island's ownership and his personal business plans of developing a small resort haven as if he has been hired to give me a private briefing on his proposal, for God's sake. If I knew him even just a little bit better, I would have told him to shut up hours ago. Instead I sit with this forced smile, feigning my interest and secretively thinking how much

I would love to just backhand him at this point and tell him to snap out of it and deal with his obvious, blatant reality.

    This sudden, spontaneous urge is not something new for me and, in fact, it's more predictable than not, I think, as I attempt to contain my surfacing impulses. I have stifled these episodes of brewing rage for years, pushing back at even the slightest threat of eruption, but, as we all know, like a rushing river once contained by a great indestructible dam, it was only going to take one small insignificant crack to blow the entire seaway wide open. In the interest of protecting Marco from any rising emotional tsunami, I distract myself from the current conversation and try to decipher the exact moment this first began as an issue for me. The day of our family trip at the beach comes back to mind and returns as vividly as if it were actually taking place again in this very moment.

∞∞∞∞∞∞∞∞

I remember the hints of green onions, the remnants of garden salad and the smell of fresh radishes that drifted from the table as I looked at the potatoes still lying sparsely in the bowl in front of me. Potatoes—the sight of their starched presence made me feel physically ill and crept into my being like an irritating presence. Meticulously, I had eaten everything around them, careful to avoid any direct contact. I hated potatoes.

    Even though prepared to culinary perfection by my father, roasted with the fresh herbs from Giovanni, our local Italian vegetable god, they still represented a choking conformity for me. Nothing could disguise their utter commonness.

My father ate them. He loved them. I watched him eat, forming my own opinions. He spent his whole life in pursuit of maintaining control, all the while incapable of possessing a single ounce of command. Spinning in a vicious lust to gain some edge, some small insignificant piece, yet unable to position a solitary foothold, he floundered like a mountain goat scrambling on a flat vertical cliff, too stubborn to admit vulnerability, too proud to accept the possibility of any alternative. Controlled by all that he feared, he worked his entire life to command the behaviour and thought processes of all around him, using dictatorship as his only means of superiority. He even took up rock climbing, claimed it was his passion. Yes, Sam could endure the fear of death in every single step, yet he could not extend to open the small mound of love within himself.

Love for Samuel was ownership, domination. Perhaps there was a moment when my mother saw something different, something more. I never did, but there must have been a hope or a promise or something.

I pushed my plate to the centre of the table that day and glared at my father. We had never been friends, Sam and I, not that I could remember. And we barely spoke at all since he sentenced me to boarding school. I hated him for sending me away and didn't speak to him unless they choked it out of me.

"That's OK, Nattie, I don't eat them, either," my mother chirped, trying to slice the discomfort between Sam and me as I stared at him, while he sat repeatedly tapping the side of my abandoned plate.

She was the eternal buffer, continually trying to bring peace between the two of us. She was afraid of my interactions with him and knew the hatred I held for him was dangerous. Honestly, I think she was silently concerned my father might not have been the only isolated case.

I glanced at my mother's plate that day and it was true—she had not taken any. Now that I thought about it, I had never seen my mother eat potatoes. No, she was a worldly woman. She knew what they were. They were death. She was not about to buy into a boring old cardboard life, and neither was I.

"Natalie, finish your potatoes," my father insisted.

"Now, we can't very well make her eat them when even I don't," my mother bargained.

"Well, maybe someone else should eat them too," he muttered under his breath, knowing what he had said.

He hoped, prayed, he could mould my mother into the wife he thought she should be. My mother was a woman unto her own laws. Everything was conventional for Samuel. This, I believe, drove my mother to be even more eccentric, provoking action that was clearly unacceptable to him.

Each summer, her friend, my Auntie Kaila, would come and stay with us for a few days. This drove my father mad. In the guestroom, the two of them would laugh, snickering like school girls, drinking wine and smoking cigarettes late into the night. Each morning I would hear my parents meet in the hall.

"Rebecca," he whispered loudly in frustration.

"Oh, Samuel, it's just been so long since I've seen her. It's only a few days," she persuasively pleaded.

My mother only called my father Samuel when we had company or when she was negotiating for a small piece of freedom for herself.

My mother winked at me that afternoon. Our eyes locked in connection. I knew I would not have to eat potatoes that day or ever. I, too, was now a woman of my own. I was excused. My aggression for my father did not vacate with the disposal of unwanted potatoes that day, however, and would go on to cultivate an entire crop of its own. An angry harvest, unfortunately, that I would eventually reap with distaste, and one I would constantly need to be pruning.

∞∞∞∞∞∞∞

That day occurred more than three decades ago now. I know that, with the length of its history alone, anger is no longer a mere thought that exists outside of me and separate; it is entrenched, controlling me from deep in my being at every given moment. Marco is merely my latest reminder.

I stop listening to him, finding it amusing how people busy themselves in the drama of their deliverance, only to forget the truth. Marco has clearly forgotten his. Over time, his complaints have served to justify his ways and to completely protect him from reality, providing everything except a direct access to the facts.

The fact is, Marco had given up a long time ago and his big fat ego was too stubborn to admit it. The only thing he chose to do now was to blame everyone else, and now that his pathetic excuses were dominating my cab ride, he had no idea just how close he was to being schooled into an entirely new, blunt version of life. I was unable to see the connection at the time, but our stories were not all that different. His was about a foreign land, and mine was of a distant father, but both refused to grant us what we truly desired. Neither of us would be big enough to admit, or even to recognize at that time, that these struggles were, in fact, nothing to do with any outside force acting upon us at all.

∞∞∞∞∞∞∞∞∞∞

The car stops at the foot of a winding cobblestone staircase. I stand at the top of its dimly lit pathway and place my hand along the railing, pausing before descending to sea level. Marco's conversation ceases for the moment, leaving me thrilled with his silence and finally allowing me space to release all the suffocating negativity I have been inhaling over the past hour. Looking down, positioned on the edge of this vast crystal blue ocean, I take in a sea of bamboo and canvas umbrellas spread over several dark wooden tables and chairs that are strategically dotted with hand lanterns. The servers move rhythmically in their casual linens and sandals, catering to the diners at a slow beat. The velvet mauve sky is just turning to slightly darker hues of the same as the sun begins to set. The air carries a soft, luscious flow of the universe that is moist and smells of salt. Eman stands near the kitchen entrance, smiling. I wave and make my way toward him.

FOUR

You have the power in the present moment to change limiting beliefs and consciously plant the seeds for the future of your choosing. As you change your mind, you change your experience.

—Serge Kahili King

Older, fifty-eight or so, Eman carries a sensual grace about him. His steady, solid movements reflect years of self-confidence and pride in his abilities. He has an elegance so tangible and compelling that it makes you want either to physically devour him or wrap yourself in him entirely. His tall black stature is flawless and strong, while his energy is soft and glowing, consistently releasing this undying stream of warm, gentle light. Unaffected by fast fads or fickle women, he is meticulous by nature and impressed only with classic, genuine, loving people.

"Hello, Eman."

"Ms. Natalie," he states evenly with his arms

outstretched to give me a welcoming hug as I unconsciously hum aloud with his familiar greeting.

He has a way of directly acknowledging a hidden place within me that even I have no access to, awakening this mute, sleeping tigress inside. I stand in courageous pride and smile as he holds me in front of him. Eman's endearing acknowledgement allows me to feel the power in my femininity. No matter what I have done to myself up until this moment, or how much I have denied myself life, right now as I stand with him I am proud to be a woman. I am sure I am not alone in this experience. Eman is an absolute master in acknowledging the true essence of a human being and allowing a person to identify what is truly at the core of his or her own heart, no matter how infrequently used.

"Shall we get to our table?" He lightly touches the base of my back, leading me toward the larger group, and holds my chair for me as I sit down and join the rest who are now waiting.

His eyes are bold, without fear or flinching. The concrete strength of their dark rounded marble grants me permission to delve deep into his complexity. Knowing that he has been a bachelor his entire life, I am certain such direct and undivided attention has successfully undressed many a woman for Eman. I don't care. He is the kind of man to whom you would sell your own soul for one moment of self-understanding. The past and the future have nothing to do with it. With Eman, there is only here and right now, with each moment serving only as this endless, unravelling exploration.

∞∞∞∞∞∞∞∞

Initially, Dane introduced us while we were both in New York. I found Eman interesting from the moment we met while in a meeting, and I watched him from across the room, taking note of his deep tan Italian leather shoes with the chocolate-brown laces. I remember thinking that if I ever bought a pair of shoes for a man, those would be the ones I would buy. He sat that day and calmly twirled a smooth crystal stone between his fingers throughout the entire meeting. In a business world so based on appropriateness, he was solid, unconcerned with what others thought. He sat and rubbed that small stone between his fingers all afternoon. No one said a word.

Being as young as I was at the time, I never thought Eman would look to me seriously, but he had. We developed a respect for one another almost immediately. Our infrequent meetings and business conversations over time only served to expand the rapport between us. Conscious more of the mental stimulus and less concerned with any age discrepancy, we enjoyed each other and shared a lot about business, relationships and life. He admired me for my passion and courage to move forward and take risks within the company. I respected him for his power and directness in life. He had an uncanny ability to see the hidden, a person's underlying intent. He heard beyond what a person was saying, to the real story of what the person truly meant. You discovered yourself in his company.

∞∞∞∞∞∞∞∞

His hand slightly brushes my shoulder as he positions my chair and sits down beside me. I take a deep breath and shake my dead heart, like a wet branch taps on an old tin roof—at first slowly until the wind picks up and then as fast as the branch will allow, with each bang consistently and repetitively rattling the entire house and all of its contents within. Although he is significantly my senior, Eman's touch rejuvenates me, making me feel like a small girl and a forbidden vixen at the same time, a duality for which a woman can only pray a lifetime. Age is definitely a state of mind, I think, as I curl my toes into the cool, white sand and bury my feet in its thickness and wish only that my life could be filled with friends like Eman, who awaken my spirit and remind me of the person I truly am.

The night darkens. After dinner, and when Eman and I have a moment alone, I ask him about the men I saw earlier in the afternoon on the boat. His response is both shocking and vague, serving now only to heighten my interest in the real answer.

"Did you know in some small towns, the police will know the town's drug dealer and his every move, but never arrest him?"

I look directly at him in silence, waiting for him to solve the inexplicable mystery he is currently directing at me.

"Under surveillance, they will watch, insanely document every piece of incriminating evidence required and then never charge him. Do you have any idea why they would ever do something like that?" he questions, twirling the dessert fork in front of him in small circles, then continues.

"Some things are better left as they are, Natalie."

I look directly at Eman, confused, wondering what he has actually just said. Is he implying that I witnessed a drug deal this afternoon? I admit it all did seem a little cloak and dagger, but I was under the impression, no matter the varying levels of organization, that drug deals were a little more inconspicuous.

"Feel like a walk?" I ask Eman, deciding to leave my questions for a time when I will have a better chance of getting them answered.

"Sure, just give me a moment," he replies as he leaves to speak briefly with the chef.

Once Eman is ready, we leave the lightened area behind and walk toward the darkness. I am tired. It has been a full day, and I am ready to go back to the beach house soon. I listen to the waves lightly lapping on the sand. Eman wraps his arm into mine, as we walk further down along the shore.

"So, how's everything up on the Coast?" he asks.

"Things are good. Starting to take a few different directions with the company, which is great. You know me; I love the challenge."

"Yes, you do. Why is it that you keep yourself so busy, Natalie?"

"What else is a girl to do, Eman?" I joke, trying to appear nonchalant.

"Let someone in," he replies seriously.

"Oh," I respond as if now listening to someone communicating in a foreign tongue.

We come upon a grouping of old, grey logs. Distinctively ancient from the penetrating sun, the logs are bleached and dried from many days in extreme heat, their deep crevices reminding me of fairy tales I have read as a child. Their surface is thick and grey; their lines, certain, much like the humungous door that I imagined the giant had at the top of the hill. In the grand old castle, his door was fit for a king, tall and wide with its grated peephole and locked handle, securing the deep, dark secret of the land, forever. I sit to smooth the aged and familiar surface.

"They remind me of fairy tales," I say, turning to Eman. "Locked castles and big, bad secrets."

"Big, bad secrets," he repeats, slowly.

"And what are yours?" he asks as he snuggles in close to me.

"Too many." I laugh lightly and look away.

"No," he utters, not willing to let me off the hook so easily. "The big one."

"What do you mean?" I say, pulling slightly away from him, automatically guarding myself.

"In all the years I've known you, you've never dated anyone seriously, for any length of time."

"Look at you—you've been a bachelor your entire life," I deflect, matter-of-factly.

"Yes, and we can talk about me later, but what is it with you?" he asks like he really wants to know the answer.

"Fear. Absolute fear," I admit with dead honesty.

"Natalie Lauren, fear?"

"I guess there's a fear of being hurt."

"You guess?"

"Yeah."

"Were you ever hurt?"

"Yeah. I was, once," I confess quietly, unsure whether I want to go where this conversation is now leading, but knowing it is one that I can no longer avoid.

Eman leaves a long silence before making his gentle but insistent request. "Tell me."

∞∞∞∞∞∞∞∞

In all honesty, I didn't think I had the courage within me, but I felt Eman's tenderness open for me like a small magic carpet that might finally be able to take me away from all of my fear. Once I found myself comfortably aboard, its security provided me with all the strength I required, and I found myself telling him a secret I had held for more than twenty years of my life, one that I had never told a soul. I knew I could trust him to listen and do nothing with the information. And I knew it was time; I just couldn't believe the words were so easily falling out of my heart and into thin air after all these years.

The truth was, I had been here before. I came down on spring break with a bunch of girls when I was eighteen. My father had been furious with the idea, but we came on our own anyway. After a few of days of hanging out and meeting some other tourists, we went with some college boys to a midnight reggae bash along the beach. We had never seen anything like it before—so many people, such great music. We danced all night. When the party started to die down, we headed up the beach and back to the road. Somehow I got separated from the girls and paired up with one of the guys from the group, who said he knew a short cut and threw his arm around my neck. At the time, I thought he was a little rough, but when I was with him alone, I saw his eyes up close, and knew he was wild and aggressive. I didn't know whether to trust my intuition and run into the dark or forget what I was feeling and try to make small talk. He didn't allow time for decision.

In one swift swing, I was down and soon never to forget that pier. I couldn't speak, I couldn't move. In my mind I was screaming for help, but in reality the sweating grip he had on my throat was so tight, I could barely even breathe. All I could do was concentrate on the burning grains of sand as they grated my skin raw. "Concentrate on the pebbles," was all I told myself. As the excruciating surge of pain ripped my body open for the first time and I felt the heavy, suffocating skin of this beast pound repeatedly on top of me, I just kept telling myself to think about the pebbles. There was nothing I could do but watch as he attacked me. There was nothing left for me to wonder.

He kept whispering in my ear, "I'm gonna fuck you, girl. Yeah, you're gonna like it." He kept saying it over and over again with each stab further splitting my body, as if he were proud of himself.

"Like it. You fuckin' like it," he whispered and hammered, taking some kind of sick pleasure in being so quiet and violent at the same time.

I had never had sex before, but I knew one thing: I might find my friends, but I knew in that moment, there was no way back.

∞∞∞∞∞∞∞∞∞∞

I sit quietly with Eman, reflecting and realizing for the first time that this was the real source of my panic around direction. This was the day I got lost. Because of my inability to navigate my own way that night, I physically and mentally suffered violently. Unconsciously I freeze every time I even think about direction again, and the anxiety immediately resurfaces to haunt me. Because I buried the vicious consequence from that day, my body automatically reacts in utter horror every time I try to find my own way. I am petrified of making another mistake and have carefully created this excuse of direction to hide my real fear.

"What happened after that?" Eman questions quietly.

"I was so cold," I answer, looking out at the ocean and watching the waves inch up on the sand.

"He took more than my virginity, Eman. He stole every piece of warmth I had in my body and left me with a haunting, hollow core. I got up, put one foot in front of the other and found my way back to the group. Never said anything, then or ever," I tell him as if this is an accomplishment.

"Natalie"—Eman exhales slowly, placing his hand lightly on the side of my cheek—"Natalie," he repeats in an attempt to crack the hard shell I had so firmly cemented around any and all sentiment.

"Wasn't the first, won't be the last," I mouth vacantly, still unable to accept any offer of compassion.

"I can't imagine," he says tenderly.

"All I could think of was the time when I was six and fell on the crossbar of my bike. How much it hurt, how ashamed I was. My father was standing there, watching, judging me. I didn't want to admit my mistake, so I didn't say anything," I explain to Eman as I stretch my left arm between my legs, rubbing my wrist and motioning like the same scared little girl from years ago.

"I should have done better. My eyes blurred with tears that day, I couldn't even see, but I kept riding on in pain, trusting I was pedalling in a straight line as the tears overflowed and dripped down the front of my face. I bit my lip hard, trying to keep myself focused. I can't make a mistake, was all I thought. I can't make a mistake.

"I remember thinking that it had taken a week for that hurt to go away and wondered how long this would last. When the scars from the sand from that night eventually faded, I told myself it had never even happened at all."

"You're still riding in pain, Natalie," Eman acknowledges.

"I know."

In my conversation with Eman I am beginning to see that it has become more important for me to protect myself from any judgment and be right about the choices I have made in my life than to be honest about how much I am, in fact, hurting. I have blamed myself and felt deserving of the consequences.

"That wasn't your fault. That bitterness you're carrying—it's not yours."

"I know, but it hasn't made a damn bit of difference."

"You're a beautiful person, Natalie. You don't deserve that much anger inside of you. Do you get that?"

"It's almost like it was transplanted that day. As if what he did lives inside of me now, like another person I don't even know," I admit, seeing for the first time how much anger has truly manifested itself in my life.

From my disgust with vile vegetables to the disgrace of my own violated virtue, rage is not only my leader, but also my trusted companion; and it has been so for a long time. It protects me from everything and everyone, taking me out of the game when I feel threatened and keeping me hidden and alone when I no longer feel safe. Its burning anger is all consuming and is the only fire I have ever truly allowed inside, the only single, solitary source of passion I know as my own.

"You need to let that go, Natalie. That is not who you are."

"But how? How the hell do I do that?" I ask as I turn to Eman, feeling honestly like I want an answer, but knowing I am only one of many; so many women have gone through so much more.

"What makes me so different or deserving?" I demand.

"Pain is pain. We all have to deal with our own. Here." Eman motions as he hands me two big fists full of sand. "Same sand, right?" he questions.

"Yes," I smile lightly.

"Take it over to that ocean and let it go. No more concentrating on pebbles and how much it's gonna hurt. You're safe now. You need to forgive yourself. There's nothing you can do to change what happened, but you gotta make the choice right now, whether you are gonna let this run the rest of your life. There's then and there's now," he says as he taps one fist then the other. "Choose."

"It's hard to see it as a choice at all. They both feel real."

"You bet they do, but you've got the power. You gotta decide if you're gonna use it. Our thoughts make our worlds, Natalie, but only you get to choose which ones rule your life."

Eman pauses for several moments before continuing. "Our wounds are helpful to all of us, for a while, at least. They lead us to our journeys. When we allow ourselves to experience these feelings and let them go, we transform our lives. We learn to heal."

"Yeah," I agree quietly, knowing it is as simple as it sounds.

It is my decision now. I am not changing the past. There is absolutely nothing I can do to alter what happened. I can only move forward from here. And as horrible as my situation was or as complex as any other I could ever imagine, I only have this moment to live for myself. There is no retribution in wishing things would have been different, for me or for anyone else. There is only here and now.

I walk to the ocean, release my fists of sand and wipe myself clean, looking at my open palms in the water and realizing that clenching is an option. I am not serving anyone by being stuck and holding onto the past. I walk back to Eman, give him a long hug and close my eyes, shocked by what has just occurred and relieved, like I have never been in my life.

∞∞∞∞∞∞∞

We make our way back to the group. I am awake now. The small gathering we left over dinner has expanded into a larger festivity with chairs arranged in front of a calypso band that now plays. I select an empty seat beside a small woman sitting by herself and order a glass of wine. Eman heads to the kitchen for a few minutes.

My mind soon becomes distracted by the woman I have sat beside. If she was here before, I did not notice her. Petite in stature with a long, white cotton skirt and matching sleeveless chiffon blouse, her thin straps reveal her tiny and attractive frame.

She is older, perhaps around my mother's age or the age my mother would have been. Her skin resembles a well-nourished layer of silk, moist and properly fed, that drapes her body gracefully. A red beaded wrap is securely tied with a knot around her waist and flowered in bright embroidered prints that lay over her skirt. Her jewellery is crystal and silver with large beads and symbolic emblems hanging around her neck. Her rings accentuate her hands—smooth, strong and determined—impressive for her delicate frame, experienced.

"Hello," I greet her.

"Hello," she replies.

"Are you from the island?"

"One of 'em. Not this one," she says calmly.

"You're just visiting?" I probe politely.

"Kinda."

"Oh," I reply without further intrusion.

"Workin'," she offers, seemingly quite distracted by the music.

"What do you do?"

"Futures, travel," she says, never taking her eyes from the band.

"Futures in travel?"

"No, travel. Tell futures."

"Oh," I reply, intrigued by her response.

I take a small sip of my wine and place the glass back on the table in front of me. We sit in silence until the band stops for a break, at which point the woman turns to face me.

"Through the Caribbean, all over. Wanna readin'?"

Fascinated, I accept, not placing any real faith in such eccentricities. I am intrigued by her, nonetheless, and place my hands in hers. She closes her eyes and awaits revelation. I watch her. Her hands are huge for her size, I notice now, as she holds mine. Fairly muscular, yet softened with the silver bands that encircle her fingers, they feel warm and magical. Of the four rings she wears, two on each hand, the one on her left forefinger catches my attention. I cannot make out its symbol but comment on its uniqueness nonetheless. With the same remoteness one would feel toward an old project that has long been on hold, she answers with a sense of detachment, explaining it as a connection to a past life. "Land of the livin'" is how she phrases it. Although confused as to what she means, I do not question her.

"Hmm, lots of promise for ya future. Recently settled something long burnin'. Openin' ya path now. Should be proud of yourself, Natalie. Ya come a long way."

Abruptly, the woman has my full attention, since I have never mentioned my name. She looks directly at me as she speaks. I swallow hard. She explains the past, the boarding school, my father, my mother and Brendan. Any lack of faith I previously held quickly vanishes. I listen as she reiterates my life story.

"Not that she was weak, your mother. Couldn't find a means of communicatin' her feelings. Couldn't deal with the pressure. You're much like her, but you're strong, indestructible. You got a power, great power. People come to you, Natalie. Lots o' luck in love and soon. He's in music. He'll introduce ya to a whole life you could have never imagined. Yep, he's the key. Whole new life. There's somethin' he can't tell ya. Ya need to remember, he loves ya. Don't judge. Things aren't always as they seem.

Business—great deal of success. Don't fall to the fear. It's the fear that limits your journey. Travel and trust. You'll find what you need."

She pats my hands as she finishes. "There ya go; hope that'll help ya on your way."

I reach to pay her, but she refuses. She stands to leave. I thank her repeatedly for her time, feeling an odd connection, yet not knowing what to do. I want to know more.

"Before I leave, it's important I tell you one more thing, Natalie. There's no good. There's no bad. All things are what we choose. No right. No wrong. Only lessons. You can't judge a person's actions. You make the same decisions. What's important is what ya do with 'em. Sometimes, ya gotta put all your cards on the table to have what you want," she says as she motions her hand flat in a semicircle, as if smoothing a table linen.

"There's a spirit protectin' ya, Ms. Natalie, a young maiden. She's waitin', sittin', no moccasins on her feet. Willin' to walk with ya, so ya feel everythin'. It's time for ya to walk with her. It's time for ya to feel. Remember, travel and trust. You'll find what you need."

At that moment she says goodbye, and Eman comes to join me, placing his hand on the back of my neck as we stand and watch the woman leave.

"Did Sofia grant you a promising future?" Eman asks.

"Possibly."

"Never known her to be wrong."

"She wouldn't take my money."

"Sofia sees more than futures. Sofia sees magic."

"What do you mean?"

"There's a very good reason she didn't take your money."

"I don't understand."

"You will. You will," he responds reassuringly, as if he knows something more than I do.

"Do you play the guitar?" I tease Eman.

"Been known to. Come, love, dance with me."

As we dance, I allow myself to be close, feeling a new connection to the moment, realizing that for the first time in a very long time I feel alive and unguarded. I feel the wind and Eman's hand in the small of my back, resting where the past has formerly wedged its dark tense direction and now where a space lies open and free.

FIVE

Loves takes off masks that we fear we cannot live without and know we cannot live within.

—James Baldwin

Relieved and somewhat exhausted from a personally rewarding, yet politically entangled, business trip I am happy to be home and attending the opera with Dane. The initial cynicism of Marco was only the introduction to a long line of business interactions in which I found a stagnant and weighted negative influence. My prior political research enlightened me about the hovering fear that still lingers in many of the islands' inhabitants, but, in the end, I was left unable to get around it.

Although occurring decades earlier, the brutal slaying of a greatly admired political leader was still a reminder that there was no room for opinion. This example of the tragic fate of someone who possessed too much of a humanistic quality confirmed that there was one way, one line of thinking, and no leeway for compromise. It was politics. Everything was politics. All were aware who controlled, where the power was held and exactly to whom they owed their pledge of allegiance, all except for me.

Left in the dark for the duration of my stay, I was unable to discover the hidden source of corruption that was undoubtedly prevalent, but someone was definitely limiting expansion. Such loyalty to secrecy, I knew, could only be based on absolute and utter terror. Whether the group of men I saw coming onto shore that afternoon had anything to do with it or whether they ran an entire entity of their own, a whole underworld of business was definitely being conducted by a grand puppeteer. I saw no evidence of strings, only dolls dressed as businessmen and women who performed in knee-jerk reaction.

The signs of domination were easily detectable, and I could sense people's fear. Fear is something that eats from the inside and, like any chronic case of bad breath, you can smell it whether they open their mouths or not. As much as I stood for the development of BPI, I did not wish to be made an example. I was of no use dead. Seeing grown men and women stand like frightened children before me during my time there, I knew one thing for certain—I held absolutely no interest in reinventing the wheel.

The warmed burning sensation that pole-vaulted through the centre of my chest and the rash that etched beneath my skin like a scarlet fever on several business occasions on the island were ample warning for me. Attuned to my own body rush of adrenaline and the terrified eyes of potential business partners, I read their apprehension. They were being bullied, controlled by insecurity, denial and deep-seated hatred. But I was committed to getting rid of the chaos in my own life, rather than collecting more.

Despite my aversion to corruption, I still find a part of myself attracted to the contradictions of island politics. I share the frustrated struggle for independence and understand the constant need to continue it. But, I also feel the allure of acceptance. After many nights of being separated and alone, one always wants to belong, regardless of any personal price. There are many nights that I, too, with every bone in my body aching, crave inclusion. With the passage of time and the opportunity to see the world from a different perspective, however, I have learned to resist the seduction of other people's approval and now know that when warnings surface, I am to adhere to them.

Dane understands this well-honed and distinguishing trait of mine and trusts my ability to differentiate between roadblocks and dead-ends. He has done some twisting of his own of late, resolving his tumultuous relationship with Hannah, once and for all, and now, too, is a firm believer in the Red Flag No Tolerance Theory.

The amphitheatre is hushed as we sit and wait for the curtain. I have never seen anyone affect Dane personally as much as Hannah did, and in the past couple of months, I have finally come to understand why.

∞∞∞∞∞∞∞∞∞

Before Julian's opening and my trip to the islands, Dane and I spent two weeks laden with meetings to gain financial buy-in on our latest project. On our closing day of consideration, Dane sat distant and distracted, while I was left making most of the pitch.

Finally on a break, and determined to get to the source of his upset before our entire day was completely shot, I rifled into him the first moment we were left alone.

"What the hell's going on with you?" I demanded.

He said nothing.

"OK . . . nothing. Great. I can work with nothing. Hell, I've worked with nothing all goddamned day." I paused and rounded his side of the table and continued.

"Just a little presentation. No big deal. Natalie can handle it. After all, just a few million bucks we're talking about. No point in you getting involved, really. Why would you? No, *really* . . . why would you?" I challenged, contracting my eyebrows in anger.

"You could just sit back and let the whole damn thing fly out the window. In fact, maybe I should save myself a whole lot of time and just throw the whole damn thing out myself."

I picked up the papers lying on the table in front of him. He grabbed my wrist as I attempted to swing my arm past him and held it firmly in mid-air.

"All right," he muttered in frustrated resignation.

"Ah, so he does speak," I replied sarcastically, knowing I had pushed far enough.

Dane sat with his legs crossed behind the large, sleek boardroom table with his fit body now twisted to one side, looking out the window. Leaning back in the large, padded leather chair, he wiped his chin and slowly tapped its rounded point with his thumb and index finger, as if beckoning utterance to surface. With a concentrated squint, he sighed heavily and reluctantly turned his hazel eyes from the window and looked directly into mine.

"I think I've made a huge mistake, Nate." He shook his head and blinked in extended intervals.

"What?" My thoughts raced.

What could have possibly happened? We had worked so hard for this opportunity to be here. What was the problem? Was he backing out altogether, and why now? I sat down beside him and leaned forward to listen attentively, hanging on every word as if gathering the last few exhalations left to modern language, knowing both of our lives depended on this.

"I don't see the point."

"Of?"

"Our involvement."

"What's up with you?"

"Nothing."

"We need this deal. You know that."

"For?"

"For? What do you think for?"

"To manipulate."

"No."

"To control, stifle . . ."

"There are compromises, Dane."

"To lead the creative to the conventional bullring, and then what?"

"I have never seen—"

"There's no intention," Dane raised his voice as he interrupted.

"Of?" I countered, just as loudly.

"Are we progressing, Natalie?"

"Of course."

"Making a difference?"

"Yes."

"I call bullshit."

Making a difference was most important to him, I knew. I prayed he had not demonstrated his manliness last night over cocktails and socked some deep-pocketed investor in the side of the head. He was adamant about his ideals. This often blinded him, however, in the face of reality. I pulled my chair closer as he began to explain the occurrences of the past few days and the reason for his agitated uncertainty. I was soon to discover that his recent and gripping entanglement held absolutely no connection to BPI or our current negotiations. Thank God.

He had been battling from the onset, feeling entirely connected to Hannah, yet utterly disjointed from the whole relationship, like a professional ballplayer at the World Series, sitting on the bench for the entire duration. He was at the game; he just wasn't in it.

"So, you're done waiting?" I asked blankly, trying to get a straight answer.

"I've been down many a road of noncommittal women, Nate."

"So, you know the signs then?"

"I'm like a fucking lap dog waiting for the next cuddle."

"Well, how long do you want to go on like that?"

"There's always a circumstance, a reason, a goddamned story."

"Doesn't sound like a mistake to me."

"Why the hell does it feel like one?"

That afternoon I sat and emphatically watched not a public powerhouse but a small child, young and terribly disappointed, recall an unforgettably ruthless and devastating morning from his memory. Hannah was only the current layer of a scar embedded much deeper. With a sad rawness, I watched Dane unravel not his breakup with Hannah, but the disappointment he had experienced as a child. His pain resurfaced and stood like a third person between us.

"My mom drank, a lot. But it was his job. He was her husband for Christ's sake. Who did he think was going to look after her?"

"He was your father," I affirmed, knowing it was one acknowledgement he avoided at all costs.

"Yeah, well, I became the man he wasn't that day," he proclaimed, proud and completely resentful.

And he certainly had. Dane Barnett was a strong and responsible man, who never left his mother and raised an entire empire and her at the same time. I did not try to fix anything about him that afternoon. I sat and listened. No one had ever heard what it was like for him, having his entire world ripped apart. He sat stilled in the chair, rubbing the thumbnail on his left hand. The motion one would use to remove an ink spot, firmly and repeatedly, applying the same routinized pressure over and over and over again. I sat and said nothing. I looked at his hand. There was no actual blemish.

"If she's so content, why's she endlessly running to her ex for support? If she's not sleeping with him, what is it? The calmness in his face, the fleck in his eyes or the way the goddamned hair grows on his arms?" he shouted, the veins rising from his temples as he tried to understand Hannah's behaviour and her obsessive connection with her ex-husband.

Reaching the point where he could no longer permit the dismissal of his own affection, he simply hung up the phone, leaving her to deal with its consequential mind-numbing tone. She called to justify and again explain, just as his father had years ago. Lies were of no value to him. Neither were the people who told them. He stopped listening.

Later that night, he sat quiet with heightened courage and saddened ink to pen the only closure of which he was mentally capable. When the courier arrived the following morning, Dane sealed the large manila envelope with regretful distaste. He closed the door and held to the finality that the security of its lock symbolized for him. Firmly and for several moments he waited, clutching, questioning his own readiness, afraid to let go of the doorknob.

"Imagine, thinking a fuckin' door handle's gonna change your life?" he commented, frustrated. "Now what?"

"That's up to you."

"It's just the first few days, ya know. After that, I'm fine," he said in an attempt to pretend it didn't matter anymore.

"The familiar's the hardest, Dane."

"There's only so much furniture you can arrange, Nate."

"Yep."

"After a while, it's all just stuff ya want to get rid of," he said resignedly.

"Yep," I admitted.

He knew there was not one action he could take to force the feelings of Hannah, to persuade her. Coercion would not grant commitment. He could change her mind for a while, but the heart knew only one path. No matter the attempt to pave its highway toward a stated goal, the heart would always return to its true desire. We both have sufficient evidence to prove that. He could create secure surroundings and buy her beautiful things, but longing was one motivator, absolute in its consistency. There were only so many objects one could possess. Regardless of their valued beauty, luxury would be unable to contain the yearnings of the heart. For such aspirations did not require the comfort of materialism, but stirred from within and searched amongst their environs to find their destined match. This wanting defined life, and Dane knew it. The hunt could not be denied.

The frustration came from the liberation Dane allowed himself with her, going further than he had ever gone. He asked only for her allegiance in return. She had disappointed him. This was not his first taste of emptiness, nor his first of emotional paralysis. He had hoped it would have been his last. Just as the small young boy craved for the return of his father, the innocence within this grown man would now pine daily for the reappearance of a woman, again awaiting an hour of hope that would never arrive.

Ceasing his obsessive behaviour, I placed my hand securely on Dane's that afternoon, relieving the heated enamel at the tip of his finger and informing him it was enough. He held his eyes to mine for a very long time before casting them evasively back to the window. As I stared into his eyes, I went beyond any physical colour or emotional pain to the real being that existed inside. What I realized in that afternoon is how easy it is to forget that we were all once children. We become grown-ups and are forced to live in our adult worlds, but until we have the opportunity to let that little boy or that little girl see the light of day, we all still carry those little people with huge disappointments inside. That afternoon, Dane took the opportunity to finally set his younger self free.

∞∞∞∞∞∞∞∞

With the first act just about to begin, Dane lightly raps his open palm on the top of my knee, before reaching to place his hand underneath mine. He smiles without saying anything at all and turns to face the front platform as the audience light slowly dims. A robust operatic tenor enters centre stage with arms outstretched. He takes a breath from the depths of his soul and begins to unravel a story of love, lust and loyalty. I squeeze the top of Dane's hand in excitement, knowing that for the time being, our respective dramas have ceased.

Once the performance ends, we quickly make our way to the exit. I have arranged for our car to be waiting outside to take us directly to Francesco's, where we are meeting for our final approval on the Newstrom account. Dane sits, staring out the window with his lips pressed together and lightly flicking his thumbnail against his bottom lip. I listen to the familiar, short puffs of his breath as they breeze over his fingers and telephone ahead to the restaurant, confirming all of our final arrangements. We sit in complete silence, in our last few minutes before judgment.

Francesco greets us upon arrival and leads us directly to the table. Apologizing for our slight delay, Dane pulls the empty chair at the head of the table and sits down. I arrange myself at the other and order us both a drink. Dane will take a single malt, neat, and for me, the usual.

The talk lightly skips around the economy and the local investment scene and slowly drifts toward the pending contracts. I note the rhythm. There is a flow when one has done business as long as we have. The dance is visual. I sit with a positive and prepared posture, confident all will transpire to our benefit. I have done my homework and although I hold myself physically clenched until their acceptance is formally announced, it is more out of habit than fear. I am not disappointed. By the time the appetizing array of Francesco's famous antipasto arrives, Dane is their man, and BPI has once again secured its contract.

From the small appetizer plate beside me, I select one of Francesco's marinated olives and chew slowly, savouring its elaborate and foreign juices, along with the secret flavour of success. Much like the taste of my mouth-watering hors d'oeuvre, as complex and as intricate as it can be, success, too, is simply a combination of a few vital ingredients and the creative talent that can bring it all together.

Francesco places his hand on my shoulder as he brings us another round.

"It's all in the focus, Cesco," I report in my familiar, matter-of-fact manner.

"It's all in the focus of your heart, Ms. Natalie," he says softly in his deeply sincere and thick Italian accent.

"You and Mr. Dane, you have the good hearts. This always makes for the best team."

Francesco leans slightly in front of me and sets my drink on the table, before continuing. "I see many things as I serve my pasta. I say very little. But these things, these things I know."

Lifting his hand now from the table, he reaches and gently moves a small strand of my hair delicately away from my face and softly pats my shoulder. I smile back at him and wonder if he is actually aware how comforting his subtle philosophies and unexpected, light touches can be.

"Grazie," I acknowledge looking up at him, realizing he is humble and frank, and a man of quiet power who happens to be very well-connected to his own tenderness.

I envy those who show caring with ease but do find that when I have the opportunity to receive small attentions from such people, a great part of me feels deeply grounded. And he is right—when it comes to business, Dane and I, we are a killer team.

At 7:30 a.m. the following day, I stop at Beanz Around on my way to the office to grab a latte and a toasted cinnamon bagel. Operated by a quiet, older couple, the café is warm and cozy like a grandmother's kitchen, with its small wooden tables and deep forest green-painted walls. Old barrels of aged wood are displayed about with black-stencilled letters claiming their countries of origin: "Chile, Mexico, Costa Rica and Peru." The depleted burlap bags haphazardly arranged on the walls serve as the room's decor, along with black and white pictures of faraway places such as Africa, India and Thailand.

A small narrow ledge outlines the front window. Above and just to the right hangs an old farmhouse mirror, aged with its backing coming to the forefront, shouting the universal lesson that all is eventually and inevitably revealed. I think back to my conversation with Eman, when he described me as a flower burnt in the bud. Feeling now revealed and somewhat rescued, I wonder how I will move forward from here.

The ceiling is deep crimson in colour with three large fans. A blackboard behind the counter outlines all the available shapes, sizes and flavours with a sign that reads, "Whole Bean Sales Here." Wouldn't that be great if life were as easy as that? If you could only look to a billboard to view choice, weigh selection and importance, and then consciously choose the items that best suited your needs, getting exactly what you want. Nothing is that simple, I think, as the man hands me my latte. I smile and drop my change in the glass mug by the cash and read the quote on the wall behind him:

"Wheresoever you go, go with all your heart." —Confucius.

I make my way to the office.

Three dozen long-stemmed ivory roses are waiting for me on my desk when I arrive. I open the small cream-coloured envelope, well aware of the only person sending me flowers today. Much later, Dane enters through the large glass doors and makes his way toward my office. In his confident stride, like a single crow walking on the grass through the park, he is scholarly and sure, solid in each step. I watch him. He is in great shape, with his routinely maintained and firm athletic frame, and he has a slight sway to his hips when he walks that makes his shoulders move in a subtle, yet slow and seductive manner. His silver-lined hair is always immaculately trimmed, short enough for business and just long enough to stylishly toss on his off time. And his eyes, his eyes are a heated hazel with a slight green tinge that would melt the ice of an igloo with even the smallest of concentrated effort. I smirk, trying to pinpoint the reason I have never slept with the man and turn back to my work.

"And who is it that has graced you this morning, Ms. Lauren?"

"As if you need to ask."

"One must never assume."

"And my favourite." I smile, looking up from my work and raising both of my eyebrows.

"That's the advantage of an experienced man, Lauren." He smiles in seduction, slowly patting the door frame twice before heading toward his office.

"Plans tonight, Lauren?" he shouts, walking farther down the hall. "You, me, Zeffo's. Eight o'clock?"

"Sure. What's up, Barnett?" I ask, wondering what great new game plan he has mingling in the mix now.

"Feel like taking you for a drink."

"Really?" I question, knowing there is certainly more to it than that. "You buying?"

"Yep." He drags out the word slowly, which means I haven't heard the entire story yet.

"I'm in," I confirm, waiting for the trickle of details just about to follow.

"Oh, and Julian might stop by and say hi," he sings in his familiar schoolboy chant, providing me with the real reason we are going to Zeffo's and the answer to why we have never had sex.

The man is relentless. I would never get rid of him.

"Great work on the Newstrom account."

"Brilliance isn't cheap, Barnett," I taunt as my voice follows him down the hall.

∞∞∞∞∞∞∞

As planned, we meet at 8:00 p.m. at the lounge. With a timely greeting and, as expected, Julian approaches our table shortly thereafter.

"Dane. Ms. Lauren," he casually addresses both of us, as if catching us by some random and unforeseen coincidence.

"Julian," Dane replies, standing and shaking his hand. "How was the trip?" he inquires.

"Quite productive, actually," he confesses in delight and turns to look directly at my lips.

"Trust all went as planned then?" Dane continues.

"Better than we initially hoped," he responds, turning to look at Dane and then back again at me.

"Mind if I join you for a drink?" he asks, pulling a chair next to me without hesitation or an answer.

There is a certain deviance about Julian, an underlying cockiness that expresses a slight arrogance or perhaps merely portrays a man who knows exactly what he wants. Regardless, it's a feature I truly enjoy. Working in a world filled with men, I so often find many polite in the areas that call for leadership and arrogant in the realms that demand accommodation. Refreshingly, he knows exactly how to manage the appropriate balance, calling attention to the situations that require his aggression, yet still affording me my own liberty and choice. I have a hunch Mr. Miras is, in fact, a very smart man. And whatever he may lack in any area of intelligence, if anything at all, he certainly makes up for in negotiating prowess. He doesn't mess around. By the end of the evening, Julian has successfully secured a date with me on Friday night, without Dane.

∞∞∞∞∞∞∞∞

We have agreed to meet at Enrico's, a restaurant located on the west side; styled with a 1920s flair, it is distinctive for its huge pillars, dense tropical plants and massive ceiling fans that slowly propel at a hypnotic pace in its large, dimly lit room.

Sitting inside its semiprivate and enchanting allure, I await Julian's arrival and realize my excitement is much greater than formerly anticipated. He enters through the front iron gate, but stops near the door and approaches a younger man sitting at the bar, close to the entrance. The man does not look familiar; he is younger, no more than twenty-five, with straight, blond hair. He is good-looking with stylish, dark-rimmed glasses that are level along the top, forming a thin rectangular shape, urban. They speak briefly and firmly shake hands. The younger man then stands and quickly leaves, bumping his hip on one of the wrought iron tables before exiting through the front gate to join a man waiting on the street. The man standing in front of the restaurant looks like Christian, the bartender I met at Julian's gallery.

Julian takes a moment to straighten his jacket and speaks briefly to the hostess, who then escorts him directly to our table. In his short interaction, I see a hint of the warrior; he is beyond cocky, someone who is vigorous and firm, yet still quiet and mysterious, and unmistakably deadly in his intent. The cues are unmistakable, and his extraneous activities have obviously been prearranged. Yet, despite consciously knowing the importance of each warning, I forget every single parading indication as soon as he stands in front of me and speaks.

"Hi. Sorry I'm a little late."

"Bit of a problem?"

"No, no. Nothing." He pauses for a moment before continuing with a completely regenerated enthusiasm, seemingly possessing a real skill in handling one situation entirely and then wiping the slate clean and moving on to the next.

"How are you?" he asks, changing the subject with a gentle smile and wide eyes as he leans in and kisses each side of my face.

"Was that Christian outside?" I inquire with seemingly surface interest, but hoping to uncover a story I am quite certain is embedded much deeper.

"I don't know. I didn't see him. Might have been; he lives over here."

"I'm good, and you?" I respond, finally answering his original question as he sits down beside me.

"Doing well," he says, smiling and nodding his head. "You look fabulous."

He sits in front of me and says nothing more for at least a minute, like he has nothing else to do in this world but look at me. I stare back into his eyes, and although no words are actually exchanged between the two of us, I feel deeply connected to him, like I know him, like I have always known him. In the next sixty seconds, three things happen. One, I become profoundly related to the power in silence and what real communication actually feels like. Two, the large mental scroll I have been previously using to furiously record any and all my running questions around Julian's history completely disappears. And three, I become entirely captivated by the man now sitting across the table in front of me.

"Tell me about yourself, Natalie." Julian lightly touches the top of my hand as he eventually breaks our silence.

"What would you like to know?"

"As you look back over your career, what are some of the important lessons you've learned?"

"I don't know . . . never thought about it really."

"Now that you have?"

"Details," I answer quickly without giving it much thought. "The smallest overlooked can break the biggest of plans," I say, obviously not listening to myself. Already believing that Julian is the greatest thing since free drinks at the blackjack table, I do not even bother to question his history any further.

Instead, I find myself concentrating on his smooth, newly clean-shaven face and the movement of his lips as his words so effortlessly free-fall from his mouth.

"I learned some of my greatest philosophies through my painting. Always like to hear what other people learn from their work," he admits, squinting his eyes in reflection.

"What have been some of yours?" I question, redirecting the conversation back to him.

"Five major," he responds, beginning to carefully list his lessons with each finger and gently moving closer to me with his lips now parallel to mine and only inches from my face. He continues, emphasizing each number and pausing between each lesson. Ironically and simultaneously, I notice even my own breath falling naturally into his rhythm.

"One, some of the simplest objects can often be the hardest to paint. Two, all colours live in all objects; each colour is in and of itself, yet all will run together to form completeness. Three, happiness and perfection can often be found in the simplest of strokes. Four, life will paint the pictures. We are merely brushes mapping our experiences to form our own perceptions of reality."

"Wow," I exclaim and take a short breath.

"And five?" I ask, smiling, impressed thus far and definitely interested in what looks to be his promising potential.

"Five, you've got to paint with all your heart for your destiny to be released."

"Is that what you do?" I probe, thinking back to the Confucius quote I read earlier in the day at the coffee shop and wondering if such a feat is even possible.

"Excuse me," Julian interrupts as he lightly touches the arm of the server walking by. "Can we get a menu, please?"

Julian has a way about him that is almost as if he is trained to carefully control the dissemination of any and all personal information, releasing his content according to his own criteria of relevancy and at his own pace and, yet, he possesses an eager skillfulness that delivers this in such a manner as not to overtly indicate or even suggest any intentional secrecy at all.

He never does, however, answer my question.

"Have you eaten?" he asks, turning back to me and moving his hand to softly touch the outside of my right knee.

"No."

"Hungry?" he taunts, raising his eyebrow and leaning closer to rest both of his hands delicately now on each side of me.

"I could eat," I respond, pursing my lips in a slight smirk, outwardly displaying the cute, full dimple depth of my choir girl enthusiasm, while inwardly struggling to restrain the now raging and ravenous courtesan who is dying to devour her next love feast.

Hours later, I find myself sinking into the depths of what I have fought so earnestly to contain. Julian is adventurous, just as I imagined, and both rousing and tender. Despite the struggle I initially experience with my own lingering resistance, his sensual reassurance allows my body and mind to fully and finally relax, liberating the incredibly burdened and lustful being I have long buried inside and ridding me of any and all final trapped patterns of protection and performance.

In discarding my elementary and outdated thoughts, once and for all, I begin to see how the old limits I once so rigidly imposed on myself have only existed in my mind and physically do not hold any real claim to my body. It is at this moment that I completely accept my inalienable right to all carnal pleasure and begin to see the incredible lie I have been telling myself for so long. The need to be loved *is*, in fact, at the core of my entire existence.

I promise myself moderation, but as we kiss and Julian reaches behind me to grab a strong hold of both my cheeks and pulls me to him, I feel our gnawing heat coax and then command, and I know with the swelling, seductive tension now rumbling so intensely between us that there will be no holding back for either of us. As he tightens his grip and slowly lifts me on top of him now, firmly squeezing every inch of me in his hands, I grant myself permission to enjoy absolutely everything he is about to offer, reassuring myself that there is nothing I will ever regret about my time spent with such a highly skilled artist. And I am not, in any way, referring to his painting ability.

∞∞∞∞∞∞∞

A strong unwavering beam of light presses into the corner of my eyes at 8:23 a.m. the following day. Lying with a gentle sense of renewal, I open my eyes and glance at Julian's naked body beside me and watch the sun gradually move in through the drapes and highlight each definition of his body. Moving my hand slowly, careful not to immediately wake him, I touch my palm flat on his back and lightly kiss its muscular curve down the middle. Softly moving my lips upward and along his well-defined outline, I smooth my chest lightly across his bare skin, making my way to the base of his neck, where I burrow in to kiss him now more aggressively. He stirs quietly beneath me, moving his legs in slow but firm deliberation as he shifts across the bed. My muscles clench tight, both in excitement and in anticipation as I follow his movement. Reaching for the side of my face and pulling me toward him, he stops to hold the back of my head in his hand and whispers quietly into the small, open space of my mouth.

"Whaddya you want, little girl?" he says seductively as he tenderly grabs a fist full of my hair and gently, but securely, clenches it tight as I move myself upward to face him directly.

"You," I respond, like an adolescent would to a high-school sweetheart—blindly, and fearful of not having anything else again.

"Natalie," he whispers much more slowly and fully cradling my face now in his hands. "What is it you want?"

I move my hands to grab the side of his hips, pulling myself on top of him, and release my breath inside of his mouth.

"You," I answer, like a woman who has made up her mind, confident and sure, and without needing a reason at all.

Later and finally out of pure, physical exhaustion, we both decide it is time for a solid breakfast. I am famished and absolutely refuse to deny any man who promises to make me a hollandaise from scratch.

"I had the weirdest dream last night," Julian says as he begins to cut the lemons, standing in my white terrycloth robe, its tangled lapel gaping to reveal his cinnamon-smooth chest and the long black artisan necklace that hangs to his middle.

He turns slightly to talk to me while still continuing with breakfast and moves about my kitchen, like a sleek jaguar masters the jungle.

"What was it about?" I ask, taking a sip of my coffee and positioning myself comfortably on top of the kitchen counter, directly adjacent to him.

"There was this long, glass chamber lying on a table with a door that opened only from the outside. Inside, the compartment was filled with water. It was clear, like an apple green colour. When I looked past the glass and the water, there was an object lying there quietly. Its eyes were wide open with a bottle in its mouth. Looking closer, I see it's a baby staring directly at me, but unable to make a sound."

"God, then what?" I question in wonder.

"I realize I'm the one who's responsible for putting this kid inside this thing. I haven't done it personally, but I have allowed myself to be distracted by this man, this pseudo-gangster-type guy, who is actually John Travolta in the dream. I am sitting impatiently listening to him as he is trying to convince me to get in on this deal with him. I keep telling him I need to check on the baby. 'No, I need to *check* on the baby.' He keeps reassuring me that everything is fine and that he has given the baby a bottle. Finally, I pull myself away to check on the baby, only to find this little kid is locked in this chamber and can't breathe. I panic.

"Furiously, I open the glass door and push back the water, never taking my eyes off the kid. God, breathe, I shout, raging madly at myself. It was a baby for Christ's sake. How could I have let this happen? I got so caught up in making a buck, I didn't even notice what was going on. I take the bottle out of the kid's mouth and wait. He doesn't breathe. He just lies there, his eyes haunting the hell out of me. Then, watching him, I realize all of a sudden that he's not real. He's actually a part of me, like the artist inside of me, or something. Subconsciously, I have allowed my own suppression and my biggest fear is I've deprived myself for too long. I just stand there and wait, like there's nothing left."

"And here I thought, I was the one with issues," I joke with him as he lightly laughs. "Are you having problems with your painting?" I ask, recalling philosophy number five from last night and the importance of painting with all of your heart, and I wonder if there might be something of significance lodged here.

"No," Julian answers and then pauses. "God, it was weird," he says, both confused and haunted by the whole thing.

"What was your first painting?" I ask a few minutes later, still watching him and wanting to know more.

"My very first?"

"Yeah, the first you remember."

"My best." He smiles with a long look of supreme satisfaction, almost slipping into his own dream world as he stirs the melting butter around the edges of the pan.

"My best," he repeats, nodding to me in affirmation.

Although unaware he was to become a painter at the time, Julian describes the first painting he created as a child. I listen attentively as he vividly describes long swathes of dense, green willow boughs. I imagine branches swinging peacefully, draped from their centre and gently whispering to the ground below, like a mother's long, dark braid caressing her child as she lifts him into bed.

Immersed in the frontiers of child play, he explains how he lay for hours with his back to the cool, shaded ground and stared through the tree's branches to see the sunshine peek through overhead. He was warmed by the glow of the huge, old tree, while its arms strategically moved to protect his innocence from the blinding sun. He describes how the whisper of its lavish branches made their own sweet song as they swayed in the wind. I can almost feel the breeze as he speaks. Although only six years old at the time, he played there for hours in his magical land under the tree's huge, forested roof that sheltered him from everything outside.

Looking directly into his eyes, I see his comfort, his contentment, but there is something else he isn't telling me. Whether entirely muted or just mellowed, there is something else, a sorrow that has been hidden from others and, perhaps, even from himself. I want to pry deeper, to break through the obvious barrier.

The moment he speaks of the willow, I am engaged. Seeing his love and the excitement of a small young boy, I realize I could devote myself wholeheartedly to loving this person. I could tolerate his tardiness, his towels on the bathroom floor and spattered toothpaste from the last brush. My unconditional acceptance comes as somewhat of a shock to me.

"Do you still have it?"

"What?" he asks, still quite distracted with the memory of his childhood dreamland.

"The painting."

"The willow? No."

"Where is it?"

"Not sure. Just one of those things, you know, got lost over the years." His nonchalance does not convince me as he cracks the eggshell on the side of the bowl and separates its yolk into the empty glass container.

∞∞∞∞∞∞∞∞

Whether object or activity, something that served to completely define another's utter existence, I knew, did not just go missing. You do not simply misplace the very priority that defines your reason for breathing. There is a point when a conscious decision is made to turn away, to allow your own distraction or to blur the focus on your true desire. Whether it is an action you cause or one instilled by another, a choice is made. Something happened. I wanted to know the story. Someone made a choice at one point in time, for fear of loss or fear of being left. I knew you did not just choose another's needs over your own, and deny your own true passion, without a very good reason. I wondered what his could possibly have been.

It had been one night, but I knew it was only the beginning of a much larger inquiry. If I had only known then just how big it would be—if I had known the degree to which I would ache—I would never have allowed sex in the first place. Accustomed to always getting exactly what I wanted, I was no longer in control. I was only inches from testing my own ability to be intimate in a relationship and from surrendering to the immensity of my mental and physical desire for one Julian Miras, painter of the willow.

SIX

Our doubts are traitors and make us lose the good we oft might win, by fearing to attempt.

—William Shakespeare

A tiny blue light shines in the sky above me, beckoning me forward. Carefully and methodically, I begin to climb. Placing my hands on the dark rock, I pull myself from the bottom. The blue light grows larger as I move upward, while the black retreats. I struggle and continue, and now only the blue light remains. I enter a magical land that is deep and rich and abundant. I have climbed to the surface. I have made it, or so it seems. The vision fades. I step back, and all is black.

∞∞∞∞∞∞∞∞∞

I awaken. Two years and nine months have passed since that first night with Julian. Before him, I was able to keep myself safe and managed, reacting automatically to whatever I thought might be expected or required to conduct an affair for a while, until I moved on. Never becoming engaged in the first place made leaving merely another action in my day. Julian never allowed for this type of preparation for the end; time with him was lived by the moment. He didn't ask for any type of commitment, and so rehearsing my exit seemed irrelevant. We took one day at a time, and I felt safe enough with that. We never made any verbal plans or promises to each other and simply found ourselves agreeing to another moment without question. What I would painfully come to discover, however, and which, of course, I am now all too well aware of, is that there should always be a question, or at least a well-contemplated choice.

My earlier apprehensions faded quickly, and although doubts still surfaced from time to time, I didn't listen. I became content being a major part of another's life and secretly accepted this sweet slice of adventure for myself. I stopped looking for a way to kill off hope or for any way out at all. To say his leaving came as a shock wouldn't be an outright lie, but the truth was, the web the two of us had unconsciously woven had become so intricate that our separation practically slaughtered me. I finally felt what it was like to be left torn apart and alone, breathlessly hanging with a hole straight through my heart. And this time, my role was not that of the immortal black widow, but of its doomed and disillusioned counterpart. Gnawed and mangled, I barely crawled out alive.

To entertain a few of our colleagues while they were in town, Dane and I had arranged a semiformal at Da Vinci's, an Edwardian mansion that had been converted into a high-end restaurant. The faded sandstone building was designed with huge archways and open-air balconies and overlooked a forested courtyard of lush greenery that surrounded the spacious cobblestone tile. The yellow lighting in the courtyard, accompanied by the glow of candlelight from inside, gave a charming, antique aura to the night, while the smell of fresh-roasted garlic swam through the air, showcasing the delectable decadence that was soon to be served. I would never have predicted that such seeming perfection would become the setting for such an ugly demise. It was the end of weeks of continuous back-to-back negotiations, so I suppose this was as good a time as any for the onslaught that was about to follow.

Julian stood, watching me from an alcove along the side of the building. When I walked over to meet him, he grabbed my hand and led me directly into a private room just off the terrace and firmly shut the large oak door behind us.

The room was empty and immaculate, with a long, white-cloaked table down its centre and stuffy, high-backed chairs positioned for twenty or more. Earlier in the day, I had sat in the same room with the maitre d' and the chef, making all final preparations for the evening. No amount of foresight could have primed me for what I was about to experience or forewarned me that this would be a setting not unlike that of the last supper.

The two of us sit down in the huge library of fine wines that are encased and properly ventilated in cabinets made of sculptured wood and pristine crystal. I watch Julian as he sits across from me and lights a cigarette, and I smell the smoke as it gradually filters throughout the unblemished air.

"When did you start smoking again?" I question him, both inquisitive and angry.

"Couple days ago." He exhales as he looks at his cigarette.

"Just decided to sit down and have a smoke after seven years, did you?" I reply sarcastically, knowing that something is definitely up with him, and I am not in on it.

"Yep," he answers slowly.

It was his thinking stick, he once described to me, but it was also a habit he had given up more than seven years ago. I want to know why—what is it he is thinking so hard about? I listen until he finishes everything he wants to say in his rehearsed speech. He isn't telling me the truth. Neither of us says a word. We sit in silence, just looking at each other—he, with a certain degree of remorse, and I, entirely infuriated.

After what seems like hours, I look away and toward the door, to find it now standing open. Someone has obviously entered the room since we have come in, and neither of us has even noticed. We have not even been distracted by another human being moving around in the same room. This is the way it was between us and has been since the very start, and for the life of me, I can't understand why he is ripping all that away from us now.

In the moment he speaks, however, and announces our new future, I retrieve the cold and untouchable shell that formerly served to protect me from this exact hard-hearted behaviour and find myself only blankly asking, "Anything else?"

Cold and detached, he responds in one flat second, as if I am already his past. "Nope."

I sit staring at a man I am not even sure I have ever known. I cannot even begin to accurately describe the emptiness in this, but the very pit of your stomach and your chest burn at the same time, and your breath, if you have any left at all, only serves to add fuel to this all-consuming fire until, ultimately, you are left with only a vacant lot of cinders that you once commonly referred to as your soul.

He continues. "I'm sorry, Nate. It just isn't meant to be."

I watch him get up and rub the corner of the table with the tips of his fingers and slowly drag his hand along its smooth cloth surface to the other end. As his pinky slips away from the linen, he swings his arm forward and walks out of my life.

I sit in silence, like a concrete statue unable to move, feeling nothing and everything at the same time. The only conundrum with this is that I can contain all of my emotions for the moment in this motionless state. I am not, however, made of stone and know I will eventually have to move. My fear is that this will be followed by the dismantling of my entire structure. He is a liar, a coward, an absolute lying coward. It was too close to everything it was meant to be.

    I decide not to go back to the condo, knowing that he won't be there and drive straight to my place outside of the city. I need my place. As I drive home, I make my greatest effort to keep it all together but am unable to see anything beyond the pain. I am unable to feel anything beyond the aching emptiness consuming my body. My tears begin to fall and, once started, plummet beyond my control. The pain is deeper and darker than anything I have ever wanted to experience—or even imagine.

∞∞∞∞∞∞∞

In the morning, I stand in front of the mirror and can barely tolerate what little remains in my own reflection. My eyes are greyed and hazed and shocked. I have been submerged into this boundless sea of sadness with no idea how to bring myself back to the surface. I have been left. I look at the decade that has been added to my face overnight and wipe my nose, which has been running uncontrollably for hours. I grab the box of tissue on the stainless steel stand in the bathroom and lifelessly make my way back to bed, thinking honestly that this may be one cave where no exit actually exists.

    A few hours later, however, Dane arrives and makes his way through the garden, letting himself in through the back door. All in the house is still quiet as I listen to him enter the kitchen and fumble through the drawers before making his way to the attic.

The attic is where I have my room, a quiet haven I have reserved for me, where I do my thinking, surrounded by all of my favourite things in a large, open space with a high-peaked ceiling that is slanted in cathedral-like fashion and lined with bamboo thatch. A soft woven-wicker floor is left uncluttered, enabling me to wander in contemplation at any given moment. The colourful handmade rugs are strategically thrown throughout and provide me with a defence against monotony—be it of decor or what goes on in my mind when I overthink. A large, imported chest intricately designed by a meticulous, indigenous craftsman sits along the wall, its wood shining in humbled pride and serving as a contrast to the other rudimentary furniture of dark-coloured rope and unfinished log. In the middle of the room, a huge bed dominates, draped with a humungous overhead canopy of lightly printed linen tapa that encloses a multitude of gigantic, fluffy pillows and white, European cotton sheets.

A project I have worked on for years, my room is a collection of items that represent all the favourite places I have been worldwide. It is my artistic attempt to recreate the same memorable experiences for myself during those times when I cannot get away but need tranquility and solace. Times exactly like this.

All these things I have purchased and placed with the hope of providing myself with a sense of nurturing and the peace of quiet oceans and serene mountain tops. My room is a space holding old friends' smiles and the simplicities of life. None of it is going to work this time. There are just some things that money cannot buy and others that objects will never, ever be able to supply.

Dane brings a bundle of long-stemmed ivory roses and quietly places them in the water in my favourite crystal vase, which sits on the sculptured stone table at the foot of my bed. I have a thing about vases, clear vases—the transparency makes me feel connected somehow. Most people only prefer the flower at the top, but I like to see the entire view, stem to blossom. I wonder if Julian ever knew this about me. I feel nauseous. Apparently he had no idea or he would have known I could handle the roots, the secrets, which obviously exist and are evidently the very same that are now exterminating any hope of a future and our moving forward, together.

With my face hidden, I lie curled like a wounded child on the far side of the bed, nestled and lifeless, where I have been for hours, unable to move. Dane enters the room and his familiar, fresh wood-spiced cologne filters throughout as he fumbles amongst my music, looking for just the right piece. Perhaps it's the familiarity of our years together or the number of times he has saved me from my vicious versions of hell or the countless occasions I have helped him with his, but we are family, and he is here, and that is all that matters now. Billie Holiday pipes softly in the background and, as usual, is the perfect selection.

I attempt with what little energy I have remaining to roll myself in Dane's direction. Limp, I stretch my arm across the bed, beckoning his warmth to my weak and depleted spirit. As he gently positions himself on the opposite side of the bed with his back resting on the Indonesian teak headboard, I slowly crawl under his arm and into his chest. There are fewer than a handful of people with whom I would admit any degree of disappointment or defeat, but with Dane I do not have to pretend to be anyone.

"Every time it rains, it rains pennies from heaven," he sings quietly.

With the palm of my hand fixed in one position, I slowly move my fingers back and forth therapeutically and pat the smoothness of his shirt. I feel stiff and dead, and only a stone's throw away from how I felt the day Brendan and my mother were killed. Julian shifted my entire reality and brought a piece of it back for a while but now has taken my world just when I thought it might be mine, leaving me unprotected and lost, again. I feel nothing inside now, just another empty crater never to be filled, and I blame him for every lousy, lacking ounce.

My fingers pat Dane's chest in an unconscious and trancelike motion as I attempt to hum along with the music. Nothing of substance surfaces, only low moans from a discouraged voice plagued with bad timing. Nothing is said between Dane and me; nothing needs to be. He sits silently with his arm lightly around me. Despite all my attempts to be strong and determined and fearless, I am unable to withhold the roaring ache inside. Dane quietly sits, holding me. Patiently, he smoothes my hair down the middle of my back and gently wipes the tears under my eyes for hours, patting them across my cheek until they disappear. Touch is the healer of all wounds. Many may believe it is time that erases the pain, but I say the genuine love of another's real companionship heals heartache, no matter how severe. When someone can honestly share your pain, without trying to fix you or change anything about you, your weighted and wallowing sadness eventually evaporates into thin air. Truly, Dane Barnett is my very best friend.

∞∞∞∞∞∞

I draw a bath later in the afternoon as Dane goes for a walk, allowing me time to respectably pull myself together before we make our way back to the city. Gently soaking each crevice of my body in patchouli and ylang ylang, I reminisce of the times Julian and I have spent here together and attempt to seek a new sense of grounding for myself. I lived before without him. The feat is not impossible, as much as it feels like it is right now.

Once dressed, I go down to the kitchen and wait for Dane. Struggling, I hold my lip stiff as I peel an orange from the small basket Dane has brought. I did not eat yesterday or today. The rind is tough as I struggle to tear away each piece of its skin. I place the first citrus segment between my front teeth and bite it in half, severing not only the fruit in my mouth, but also the courage it has taken for me to get here. Just as the juice releases itself from the orange, tears again squirt from my eyes as I slowly force an exaggerated and mechanical chew. My face reddens as my tongue tosses the orange aimlessly; it feels offensive and terribly out of place. I force myself to swallow it and drop in resignation to half lie over the granite counter of my kitchen island. Exhausted and once again disheartened, I cover my face and cry. Why did I need this lesson? What is the meaning of all of this?

Dane returns from his walk. He brought someone with him earlier in the day to drive my car back, and we now head back to the city together. As we drive through the country, I watch trees pass, and leaves, all becoming one large green blur. I want an end to this. My face is hot, blotchy from the late afternoon sun shining through the window, only emphasizing the fact that I have been crying for at least eighteen hours straight. Dane places his hand on mine and squeezes tightly. I cannot even respond. I watch the land pass and wish for any world other than mine and question purpose and pain and the pricks that tend to come and go in my life.

"How did you find out?" I finally ask Dane.

"Julian called."

"Oh, that was nice of him," I say, clearing my throat, uncertain whether I am being facetious or not.

Once we arrive at my place, Dane opens the entrance and brings my bag up to the condo for me. I go straight to my room, change into my bathrobe and crawl into bed. Dane arranges my laptop and work files in my office and later comes in and sits in the chair beside me. Resting his elbows on his knees, he leans forward and listens.

"I know this sounds insane, but I don't know how to live without him," I openly admit. "All those years on my own, I was perfectly fine. Not even three years with him, and I've completely lost all instructions on how to live."

"I know, darlin'. You don't have to figure it out right now," he assures me as he reaches and wipes the stray strands of hair across my forehead.

"Good, 'cause, honestly, I don't think I can."

Dane hugs my hand between both of his palms, folding his fingers securely around mine, making me feel safe and supported.

"Sweetie, you can do anything. Just give yourself some time," he whispers.

"Yeah," I answer, unconvinced that any further resilience remains or that I could muster the ability to generate any at this point.

Dane stands and lightly kisses the top of my forehead.

"I'll go and let you rest. Take time for you, OK? Call if you need anything."

The next thing I remember is 4:03 a.m. shining on the alarm clock beside my bed. I lie awake. My space is muddled, unclear. I twist my ring under the duvet and turn to my side. Nothing else moves. I look around and adjust my eyes over the prearranged objects. I look to the sofa, the table and the bookstand, scanning the titles of each book and the entire collection that stands to define who I am. I have chosen each intentionally, arranging a world of knowledge around me to create the aura of educated thought, and here I lie, stunned.

Trained to handle the ever changing circumstances and responsibilities of an entire corporation, prepared to cope in all situations, and I lie naked in a robe and in a bed with no answer. There is not one book that can give me what I need. This darkness is not something that I am going to tame. There is no manual for this. It is the first time the dark feels lonely to me, and I have no strength to manipulate my own way on this one. The room is black. I feel blind and fuzzy and realize the recurring vision I so often find in my dreams has become my reality. I was at the bottom with no hope of blue, finding only black—deep, dark and sinking black. I lie sad and quiet and alone in complete darkness.

I am responsible for this entire mess; this is *all* my fault. I feel the wetness again drip down the side of my face and rub the tears away as they pool under my eyes. The reality is blatant and cruel. I have no idea what to do now. I quietly cry, pressing my face deep into the pillow. I am alone, absolutely and entirely alone. Finally, I have everything I have ever wanted and now that I am here, nothing inspires me—nothing. My entire life, I have run—in fact, have specifically searched—to find this exact place. Now that I am here, I have nowhere to go.

Daylight eventually comes and, with it, a day I fear will not pass. Anxious and insatiable, I fight with myself for its entire duration, unable to feed the emptiness or the edge. My sadness escalates to the point of anger and then crashes to deep remorse. I feel no sense of purpose or attachment to anything. Sunday. I hate Sundays.

There is nothing I can do to alleviate the alienation, no connection I can see that might bind me to another person. I want to feel home, a sense of belonging, a reference point to something, but I can't feel anything. The reality that seems to be surfacing and pointing all arrows directly my way is that I am incapable of loving.

All the evidence is here, having spent the majority of my intimate relationships forever standing at the corner of hope and loyalty, thinking it would be enough and vanishing at the first opportunity an exit arrives and before any other real truth can surface. It's quite possible that I have learned loyalty instead of love. Yes, in loyalty I was able to follow the rules and stand stubborn enough to commit to something I believed in. I could base action on facts and legitimacy, creating clear foundations and structure, where there was a reason to stand for something, but with love there was nothing tangible, nothing concrete. I needed evidence, something distinct and definite. That must be it; I have learned loyalty instead of love. This is the real reason Julian left. I don't know how to love. I reach for comfort.

For fear of accepting my true, demented and insufficient self, and edging beyond the struggle, I choose to push it down. I let my inhibitions slide into the darkness and blame myself. I have spent years hiding, only permitting relations that I knew would not grant success. I thought this had been different. Instead of allowing myself to feel the depth of this devastating failure, however, I sit now and attempt to drown any further feeling at all. Like a beaten woman, I now wish only to conceal the truth. I don't want to know the truth. I retreat to the familiar and hard.

Quietly standing in the middle of the kitchen with my third glass of a well-aged Bordeaux, I have listened to every possible heart-wrenching love song from Nat King Cole to Bon Jovi. It is now time for a little Marvin.

"Every road has to end somewhere . . . We've come to the end of our road."

I sing along and attempt to convince myself, once again, that none of it was ever real, none of it really matters, and absolutely nothing, *nothing*, will ever change. My mind keeps flipping, however, between this concocted resignation and what it was really like when Julian and I first started out.

I think back to our nights in his studio, where I would lie as his canvas while he adjusted the light. Dark, his eyes were ravenous and deep as he looked inside of me. Naked from the outside in, he saw me, and I let go. He would gently trace my body with his hands, carving me like a well-preserved Rodin. He was a true artist, always allowing for shape regardless of form, permitting time for natural evolution, no matter how long the truth took to surface. I travelled with him, believing him, trusting him and beginning to know myself, and what I truly wanted as a woman. It was the first time I felt complete with myself—no judging, no thoughts, really, just open and in wonder.

∞∞∞∞∞∞∞

In my desperate attempts to feel better about his leaving, I blamed Julian, but the truth is, he was patient. There was not one single thing he had forced, nor a moment where he did not find beauty and the opportunity to create. Reality for him was constantly unfolding. His hands were purposeful, knowing their exact skill and desire, yet waiting for the passions inside of me to be released.

I had never been with a man who truly knew what he wanted or with one who could wait for me to understand my own needs. It amazed me how his touch, something that existed completely outside of me, could mould so many years of my own denial into this warm and understanding acceptance of myself. Every time his hand smoothed the inside of my leg, he studied, to know, to feel, to accept every corner of darkness I was so afraid to admit. I felt a maze of tangled trauma simply lie still and surrender with him. I had never felt passion to the depth he inspired. His touch was always confident and provocative, discovering with every moment and unravelling this person inside of me that I didn't even know existed. Not once had he performed; every solitary second with him was connected, entirely rooted and real.

Previously, I had known only takers and, often, found it difficult to release the past from the occurring, never realizing I was actually the one unable to let go. I had often promised myself I would trust, I would commit. But I suppose this came from a need for acceptance or, perhaps, a hidden longing to know love. In being honest with myself now, I could see how easily I used loving someone as a way of escaping myself. My attempts to gain approval only left me frozen and unable to truly identify what it was that I wanted. Before Julian, I had never allowed the space in my life for wanting. I permitted necessity but never actually created a life where my desires could be identified, let alone fulfilled.

Without words at all, Julian led me through each of these steps, allowing old barriers to be and then to fall. As he moved over me, he outlined the beauty of each stroke and the power I held within my own existence. He enlightened me and taught me how any denial, no matter its form, was not only an injustice to myself, but also to the world.

Is it any wonder I was a mess? I did not want the pain to leave. It was all I had left and I wanted it to stay with me, nestled inside. I wanted him. I wanted all of him, back with me. He was mine and, frankly, I did not know any other home. He was my base. I could still feel the smoothness of his skin and the size of his body beneath my robe as he hugged me over coffee on that first morning together.

He shook the core depths of my being and altered my entire understanding of reality and order. He transformed everything I had ever known before. With each moment entirely created from nothing, he tapped this well of passion and desire I had buried so deep that I was scared to move forward without him for fear action would carry no meaning, afraid of living and of life being nothing. One did not go back. One did not find a replacement.

∞∞∞∞∞∞∞∞

I fill my glass and continue to create a sense of well-being for myself, to quiet the noise in my head and create a comfortable space of cynicism, where I am familiar and dead. I slide down the side of my kitchen island counter and sit on the dark green marbled floor, my legs stretched out in front of me. Like leaves that fall in the autumn, I sit on my forest floor, saturated and awaiting my own trampling. No one is here to rescue me now, and I have made certain of that.

Eventually I get up, place my wine glass on the counter by the sink and make my way to the bedroom. I stop and stand in front of the full-length mirror that hangs on the wall in the hall. I look closely and see the years that have been added to my eyes, lines that have crept in with no warning of their arrival. I look beyond and inside to see a small and scared little girl standing there. It has been so long since I have been able to see her. I reach for her, placing my hands on the glass and begging her to come to me, but she won't come. My fingers slide down, slowly in defeat, leaving their tracks on the smooth, flat surface as I lean back and watch her tears fall. I just stand and watch her cry, incapable of doing anything at all. I wonder at what age it was I actually left her on her own. When was it I left her alone?

I have failed her, terribly. I know the sadness, the disconnectedness, the pain and how much life I have denied her. I am responsible for her. I want to help her and make it all better and, yet, I know I cannot go back. This guilt, of which I am unable to let go, is not only creating each new moment of my life, but also destroying it.

"It's OK," I finally whisper to her.

"Everything's gonna be all right," I tell her as I watch her fade further and further away.

I know she doesn't believe me. There have been too many times I have left her behind and too many times I have lied. God grant me peace. Allow me to let her live in a way that best serves her. Allow me to choose a way that sets us both free.

My legs crumble beneath me as I sink in surrender. I am unsure at this moment what it would take, but I know we are going to find our way, together.

Later, and after what seems like hours, I get up, take one last look in the long, silver glass mirror and make my way to bed.

SEVEN

These things move within you as lights and shadows in pairs that cling. And when the shadow fades and is no more, the light that lingers becomes a shadow to another light. And thus your freedom when it loses its fetters becomes itself the fetter of a great freedom.

—Kahlil Gibran

I awaken in the middle of the night and scramble across the nightstand for a pen, knocking my watch to the floor. Time stops for the moment. I lie quietly and take a deep breath, feeling fresh and newly vulnerable. I have survived what mystics for many years have commonly referred to as "the dark night of the soul," where I have fought to face the darkness of my own existence. I have felt with no sense of purpose and no understanding of reason. I have passed through the void and risen to the dawn. This journey has taken months, but I have made it. I am alive.

I lean forward to write down every last detail from my dream and mark this moment. I know if I do not take the time right now, by morning any glimpse of new hope will be gone, erased as quickly as yesterday's lesson on a classroom chalkboard. I record everything that still lingers.

The horse gallops, thundering forward through the wet early dew. I hold the reins in my hand, smelling raw leather. The mist on my face is warm as I move over the open meadow. I am alone; silently my body rocks in the saddle. I ride, connected to the newness of the morning and its beginning.

I reach down and rub the neck of my companion, swaying with his movement. He is strength and endurance for me and signifies intent, determination and power. I know nothing of what the next moment will bring, but trust him to carry me forward, to places I cannot get to on my own.

I have overcome. There is a victory. I begin to feel the opportunity available. I begin to feel my own power. Life is opening her path. I am ready now to accept her abundance. The waiting is over. I reach to the higher powers that possess me, no longer holding to the stories that have once dictated my life.

I stop on the edge of the meadow and pull a pussy willow, a token for my new beginning. I continue to ride on for several hours and later arrange the willow in the centre of my room as a reminder of the moment when I reached beyond utter contentment, on a cool, crisp morning, alone

> *in the meadow with my stallion. I have trusted him, and he has led me directly to myself.*

∞∞∞∞∞∞∞∞

Returning my pen to the nightstand, I watch the moon disappear behind a cloud, leaving me in complete darkness. Moving to the armchair near the window, I look out onto the water glimmering in the black, bashful air, comforted now in the dulled unknowing silence and listening only to the night wind gently bringing its waves to the end of their journey, to retire silently on the shore. A chapter of my life is over. I can now admit it. Julian is gone. The clouds shift and the moonlight returns, casting a single enlightened path on the ocean. The clear beam reminds me of when my life was once simple and straightforward, and directed only with one single vision. It all seems so far away now and, yet, surprisingly so close.

I still miss him. Nights like this I crave him, in fact. Julian led me beyond any former history, allowing me to feel my own being and experience who I truly am.

I have busied myself over the past few months as a way of distraction, but on nights like this, when a dimmed light wakes me in the darkness, I sit naked in the huge armchair in front of the open window and ache, beg from the very core of my being for him to come home. I will never again feel a lover like Julian. I am certain of that. I will never know that deep liberation that trembles from inside, like a wild jaguar that has been caged in the middle of the jungle and is suddenly released. I will never again know what it feels like to be free. He was the one, the only one that was like a harbour where both my lessons and results were always aligned; the only times when I ever truly let go were when I was with him.

Tomorrow will be here in a few short hours. I will meet Dane about the Dubois proposal and bring the dawn of a new future to both BPI and to me; I will make sure of it. I will once again reclaim my infallible mask and carry on, concealing all personal issues and moving forward with mastery and intent. I need to get out of the city now, to take the time to recommit myself to the one area where I have never failed. I will go back to the life I have always known, where the mask will be my voice, where emotion is again separate, and where time continues to wear on.

∞∞∞∞∞∞∞∞

In the late morning, I drop by the deli to grab a bite before heading to the office. Dane and I are meeting at 1:30 p.m. to discuss all final details for my trip to Isla Mujeres.

Jasmine and I have spent the past few weeks in communication. Already, I have learned many things, including some of the history of the island and the theories of how its name first came to be.

There were many who thought the Spaniards had first named the island at the time of their arrival, when all the local men were busily seeking their fishery fortunes at sea, and they found only female inhabitants living there. Some felt it was the influence of Ixchel and the large number of female Mayan statues that were worshipped by the people during that time, while others believed the island gained its name as a secluded harbour for infamous pirates who safely stowed their female companions on its land while they pilfered the Caribbean waters. Whatever the true origin was doesn't really matter. I want to go and discover something new for myself and seize what I know is going to be the next bestseller for BPI. Intrigued by the mythological belief that this island was once ruled by the Mayan goddess Ixchel, I'm excited to make the trip and gain an understanding of the island and, more importantly, its people, to know and, I hope, to purge any and all remaining impurities from myself and to create a rebirth of my own.

It is Jasmine's belief that to initiate any story with one's life as a child is futile and uninformative, for only as adults can we piece together the accumulated circumstances of the past to understand our true meaning. Although our answers are so often found as a result of the events that occurred in those first few years of life, only after living through them, and through our own later experiences, can we ever discover the lessons we were meant to learn. I agree with her philosophy that to begin any personal narrative at conception is senseless, for only after years of analysis can we ever completely comprehend the genuine reason for each of our journeys. And, as I have learned myself over time, sometimes it takes this type of misguided suffering to wake us up. I can barely wait to meet her in person and get the real story. Perhaps it is the past few months and Julian, or the past few weeks in conversation with Jasmine, that are sparking my keenness to leave. But, for whatever reason, I feel an instinctive pull to this little tropical island, and I am glad the time has finally come for me to go.

∞∞∞∞∞∞∞

Dane arrives early and plunks himself down in front of me on the other side of my desk. We make all final arrangements.

"Are you sure you are up for this, Nate?" he questions once more, still holding himself in some way responsible for everything that happened with Julian.

"Yes," I answer quickly and almost adamantly, knowing the ease I feel and the skill I possess in placing all business before any personal matters. It was a given, and I was definitely going.

"Nate, there are a lot of writers. You don't have to go all the way . . ." he says, lifting his head and leaning forward toward me.

He wants to hold my hand in a quest that he knows I have to experience on my own. I may have designed it so it appears that the company needs me more than I need it right now, but we both know the truth and are well aware of what must happen.

"Everything's fine," I confirm. "I'll leave late tomorrow, spend the night in Cancun and be on the island first thing in the morning."

I finish a few last-minute details before packing it in for the day and get ready to leave the office when my phone rings.

"Natalie, here," I answer quickly.

"Natalie."

"Eman." I pause, feeling immediately connected as if he is in the next room, rather than on the other side of the continent. The man is a saint.

"I hear you are off to Mexico," he says.

"Yes, finally," I reply with long-awaited relief. "It is so good to hear your voice, Eman," I confess.

"Just wanted to touch base before you leave."

"Thank you. Believe me, I'm fine. Nothing a little time by the beach won't cure," I respond, well aware Eman knows the degree to which all this has actually affected me.

"Remember, it's all about the intention," he offers.

"Yeah, I've learned a little about intention over the past few months."

"I'm not talking about Julian, Natalie."

"Thank you," I calmly respond, knowing Eman is only trying to redirect my energy into a more positive direction, to have me look at being the cause of my own life, rather than at the effect of someone else's, and to focus on what I want now and align it with my own new direction.

"You have to believe."

"I believe, Eman. I'm just trying to figure out in what at this point," I humbly admit.

"You'll get to it, darlin'."

"Thanks for checking in," I say in deep appreciation.

He is a spiritual guru for me, forever standing in the thickest of the thick, deep in the middle of the jungle, always gently waiting and guiding me to the one path I need to pursue next.

"You've got the power, Natalie."

Later in the evening, I arrange my clothes neatly, packing now with excitement and anticipation of both loss and discovery, knowing this is going to be a transformational trip for me and ready, now, to separate from all that has happened and to commit to what it will take. And it is going to take something, but I am ready for the next level.

Eman is right. It is all about my intention now and focusing on my own creative energy. It is time to stand up and become my own warrior, to choose my own personal path and what is real for me, rather than constantly listening to the endless, idiotic cycles in my mind and recalling the past mistakes I have made. It is time to let go of limiting beliefs and decisions I made a long time ago and to now make a real commitment and be myself. I have a purpose in this world, and it is time to step up and find out what that is and make it happen. It is time to deliver.

I fasten the lock on my luggage and set it on the chair by the door; I pat its surface in the same smooth direction and place my passport on top.

Tomorrow will be an entirely new journey, forward.

EIGHT

When we are in this state of being where we are open to life and all of its possibilities, willing to take the next step as it is presented to us, then we meet the most remarkable people who are important contributors to our life. This occurs in part through the meeting of our eyes; it's as if our souls instantly connect, as though we become part of a life together at that moment.

—Joseph Jaworski

The long blare of a dull, muffled ferry horn sounds as the cab drops me off near the front ticket office at Gran Puerto, where I am to catch the ferry to the island. I buy my round-trip ticket and rush to catch the boat, which is now moments from leaving. Quickly, I hand the waiting attendant my ticket, while another takes my luggage and stows it snugly underneath the storage area at the back. Ensuring all is secure, I climb the iron staircase to the upper deck and take a seat along the side, to have an open-air and unobstructed view of the island. I lean forward and look over the railing as we take off, watching the bright turquoise water lightly churn and turn its white foam.

The day is brilliant, getting hot even at this early hour. As the boat begins to slice its path through the open water, I feel several similar and repetitive waves toss an ocean in the pit of my stomach simultaneously. It is only a twenty-minute sail across the bay, but I feel as though I am entering a mystical world of new adventure, where the beauty of its crystal-clear ocean is like a butler at its entrance, removing the dark cloak I have worn and trusted to get me this far. I take off the beige silk sweater I am wearing and tie my hair back, almost instantaneously feeling the sun burn a new existence into my skin.

On the other side, we are greeted on the dock by a swarm of local men in cargo shorts and white-logoed t-shirts who are selling island snorkelling tours and fishing trips. Although such excursions are definitely on my list of things to do while I am here, for now I hire a taxi driver to take me to my place and drop off my bags before I find Jasmine. The directions I have are vague, but the island is small, and I know she works at a restaurant on the north side, along the beach. Confident my taxista knows just where to go, I sit back in the swelling heat as the car follows the island's perimeter and winds through the crooked streets to the restaurant. A string of thatched huts and dive shacks align the ocean's edge; a painted cement building, deep pink in colour and accentuated with tree-green trim, stands out at the end of the wide sandy trek, and is, I assume, where we are headed. Reaching the end of the road, the driver stops and announces, "Santos." I pay the young man my pesos and step out onto the sand-covered cement street in front of the restaurant.

The entrance is large and open, layered with palm leaves and the smell of hot ocean and fresh cilantro. I walk through the terra cotta tile foyer, where a man sits as front host, distinguished by the encasing of gold that surrounds his left front tooth, which he bares proudly when he extends his warm and infectious greeting.

"Hola, buenas dias . . . Jasmine, por favor," I request, fumbling with my practised but unperfected Spanish.

"Ahh, senorita," he resonates in a jig-like fashion, almost making my request into a song, as he points past the tables, cloaked with their green woven cloths and thin stripes of bright orange, blue, white and yellow.

Amidst the grouping stands a woman not more than thirty-five. Tanned, her body is thin, attractive and petite. Her hair, almost mid-back, is sandy brown with natural highlights of auburn and blond; it is smooth in texture with a natural wave throughout, the kind granted in temperatures of intense humidity.

"Buenos dias, Natalie Lauren," she speaks clearly and slowly, while a huge smile expands across her face as she walks toward me.

Spanish is her second tongue, but not noticeably. She brushes her hands over the white apron tied tightly around her small waist and stretches her arms out toward me. Tremendously relieved at my own arrival, I find that her arms provide a warm and generous welcoming. Gently, she takes both of my hands, holds them in front of her and squeezes tightly.

"Finally, Natalie, you've arrived," she acknowledges, greeting me again with her tender and cheerful enthusiasm.

I look to the healthy, reddened glow of Jasmine. Innocent, she appears full of life and ready for the next adventure. I feel worn beside her. She carries a genuine wholesomeness, a clarity that makes life seem effortless and enables choices to be made with ease, appropriately, as if there exists but one answer. Her face shines. As much as I have left unattended, I am reassured—I have made the right choice in coming. She motions me to the ocean's edge, to the table she has ready for the two of us, with fresh-cut papaya and mango, along with freshly squeezed orange juice and hot Mexican coffee. We sit to enjoy our breakfast and work for the duration of the morning, outlining all we will need to cover from a business standpoint over the next few weeks.

∞∞∞∞∞∞∞∞

"OK, Natalie, let's take a walk now and go have lunch on the beach," Jasmine announces around 1:30 p.m. "Your first day on this gorgeous island cannot all be about work."

I am in full agreement. We walk along the beach and back to the bay side. I am impressed with the island from what I have seen so far. Although there are many tourists and a lot of foreigners who now live and work here, most are those who appreciate small huts and dive shacks, as its small fishing village charm still remains, despite its many recent developments since Hurricane Wilma. Crossing over and up to the street again, eventually we come upon a wooden Caribbean shack right on the water that is painted bright orange and yellow, and has fresh-cut coconuts for sale out front.

"Coco-locos," Jasmine explains as we enter through the front doorway.

"Only gets loco with a whole lot of rum." She laughs as she widens her eyes.

We walk through the open-air, awning-shaded area of the restaurant, passing the kitchen to the right and moving through several small groups of diners enjoying their lunch, to a table that is free, right in front of the ocean.

"You'll find the pace a little different here," Jasmine explains.

"Yes, I can see where there might be a couple of gaps. We certainly don't have many restaurants with sand floors where I come from," I remark as we take our seats at the red plastic patio table in the sun.

Our server soon arrives with a basket of hot, crisp tortilla chips and a small bowl of fresh salsa and places our snacks on the table in front of us. After questioning me on my seafood favourites, Jasmine automatically, and without seeing a menu, orders us two freshly squeezed lemonades with mineral water and a large shrimp ceviche to share, with a side of the very hot *habanero*.

"Pico de gallo," Jasmine explains, is the name of the freshly diced Mexican salsa we are about to eat.

She scoops a heaping spoonful onto her tortilla chip and takes a pinch of salt into the palm of her hand, sprinkling a small trickle onto her salsa and tossing another over her shoulder. She then lightly brushes the rest from her hands and takes a bite of her carefully prepared appetizer and continues.

"The pace I'm talking about, it's not just because it's a Caribbean island. It's woven in the culture here. The Maya are people who are deeply committed to balance in life. They believe we need harmony in all areas of our life, and imbalance is the root of all evil. This applies to individuals, to society and even to the planet. When we don't have balance, we suffer. And if one suffers, we all suffer. The whole point is to always be putting yourself into harmony with the universe."

"Sounds like we could all use that motto," I offer.

"Exactly. And here, we do. We work and we enjoy. And you, Ms. Natalie, I think we'll need to spend a little more time on the enjoy side of things to get you balanced out. Don't worry. It's not hard to learn here. It may be a little tough for you when you go back, though." She snickers and blinks her long eye lashes directly at me in a kind yet subtle warning.

As I watch Jasmine smile and look into her eyes, I see a sparkle of profound wisdom and a gentle easiness. Although I was here as her editor to further her career and secure our next book deal, I have a deep sense that Jasmine Dubois is someone who is going to expand my life.

We confirm all the logistics for our first week and then sit back with our lunch and relax in the sun. The ceviche is made of shrimp fresh off the boat this morning, and the best I have ever tasted.

Once we are finished with our lunch, we leave the restaurant and step back onto the street as Jasmine announces the next compulsory item on our island agenda.

"OK, now it's time for your first lesson in balance."

"That wasn't balance?" I question, knowing it's rare that I take the time for lunch at all, let alone an hour-and-a-half span not completely consumed with work.

"That was your work and your nutrition. Now it's time for some fun. We're gonna go meet a great friend of mine, and he'll make you one of the best margaritas you've ever had in your life," Jasmine promises and smiles.

I truly enjoy her attitude to life; she is on-task and accomplished, yet so unattached, just light and free to be present in each moment, not to mention a lot of fun—exactly the energy I need to be immersed in right now.

We walk farther along the sidewalk, passing the artisan vendors and another sand-floored restaurant adjacent to a small, open waterfront area. Shaded by several palm and tropical leafed trees, the beach here is lined with a few small fishing boats anchored in the ocean out front, with a couple of older ones upside down and lying on the sand. A handful of local fishermen gather around an old wooden table under the trees, cleaning and selling their fresh catches of the day, while a man works under a large, dark green canvas umbrella at another busy coconut stand next to the street. Jasmine waves a big hello to all gathered there, before we cross the road to a hotel right on the main strip. We climb the white-painted stone stairway, outlined by huge twisted tree trunks, enter the open-air lounge and take two empty high-back stools at the bar.

"Hola, mi amor," Jasmine joyfully sings as she enters and bounces behind the counter to give the bartender an affectionate greeting.

"This is my friend, Natalie Lauren. She's going to publish my book."

"Oh, berry nice to meet you," he replies with a wide and pleasant grin. "Jasmine is a good writer," he confirms, still smiling.

"Yes, a very good writer," I acknowledge.

"Dos margaritas especial?" he suggests. "A celebration today, no?"

"Absolutemente, mi amor," Jasmine sings in her endless enthusiasm as she hops to take the remaining empty seat beside me.

The bartender scoops a small shovel of ice from the cooler and into his glass shaker on the ledge of the bar and begins to prepare our drinks; he places each on the thick grey stone counter in front of us once they are ready.

"You make the best on the island, mi amor," Jasmine claims as she winks at him.

"Ahh, gracias senorita," he responds, slightly blushing, well aware of his fine-tuned skill and obvious popularity.

Jasmine holds the side of his hand with much respect as she thanks him and takes her drink, before turning to me.

"To stories yet to be told," she toasts.

"To stories to be told," I agree as we lightly touch our Styrofoam glasses packed with ice and filled to their well-salted brims.

The margarita is, in a word, delicious—not too sweet, not too tart. With good rock salt, more than a generous pour of Don Julio and a drop of Grand Marnier, it is ice cold and definitely worth the wait. The afternoon is stifling, and we quickly move from the lounge area to the pool and sit with our legs submerged in the cool, refreshing water.

"What made you give it all up and move here?" I ask Jasmine, leaning back in the sun, wanting to get a sense of what it took for her to make such a dramatic life change for herself.

"The only thing I gave up was the feeling I was living the wrong life."

I watch Jasmine as she begins to explain her previous life in Chicago and the true imbalance she had personally felt there, reminding me so much of myself and what I, too, have been tolerating and pushing under the table for so long.

"It was a struggle for me to get here permanently. That was the problem. I spent so much time struggling, I forgot any other life could even exist," she explains.

"I have a recurring dream very similar to that," I confess.

"And what happens in your dream?" she asks.

"I'm in the bottom of a cavern. I spend every day seeing the sky above me, knowing it's where I want to be. Struggling, I find the one path that will lead me to freedom and then climb to reach the top. But, as the darkness fades, I discover the walls have become these familiar landmarks I can no longer live without. Instead of allowing myself the freedom of the unknown and moving forward, I simply throw myself to the bottom and start over."

"The progress gets tainted, doesn't it?" Jasmine responds.

"Yes, it certainly does," I agree.

"Hope serves as a rival for people. You can always count on someone pissin' in your bowl of nuts," she says as the bartender places a white ceramic saucer of salted peanuts on the small, square patio table along the side of the pool behind us.

He shakes his finger from side to side and smiles.
"No, mi amor, peanuts solamente. Limon y sel nada mas."

Lime and salt, nothing more, he declares, rather amused with himself and his timely delivery. The three of us laugh together at his fitting entrance, but in all seriousness, I do understand what Jasmine is saying.

The world seems to be engrained with this negativity and insecurity. People choose to live through these jaded eyes of jealousy, with envy taking the place of any possible enlightenment. Those of positive mind are continually engaged in the uphill battle, swiping and clawing with each stride, fighting those who are deathly fearful of advancement and dreadfully determined to hold others back. Misery's not only a part of life, but it's also the beloved. Coupled with the bedfellows of resignation and hopelessness, it doesn't provide any real playground for optimism.

No matter the degree of soul searching you spend on your own, it only takes an hour at work with a mate who hates his job. It's not your fault he's ruined his life and is too weak to initiate any change, but he will try to redirect the blame and make you pay for his pathetic, irresponsible behaviour. I think back to my interactions with Marco and know, for a fact, that it's true. No matter the progress you personally make, it only takes one haunting reminder to reinstate the negative roles of the past. Well aware of the irrelevancy in your response, you sit and say nothing. As an emotional washboard, you permit the repeated scrub of old patterns to reveal your unavoidable, obligatory roles and your future. Idly, you stand and accept the scour of a harsh reminder, your guilt-ridden allegiance to dysfunction and the futility in your dismal existence.

"The problem is, people can't see all things are a part of them. Unable to accept this part of themselves and humanity as a whole, they sit negative, in judgment and in denial. That's exactly where I was at, and I didn't want to be there anymore," Jasmine explains.

In our conversation, Jasmine and I inch closer and closer to all the issues I have so carefully hidden in my own life, addressing the scarcity, the struggle that undeniably drives my own idiotic behaviour and the world, in essence.

Both Jasmine and I agree, we live in a world where people are consumed by a universal competition in a race defined by finite abundance. Once thrown into this high-stake survival of the fittest, so many envision a supply of prosperity that, once depleted, holds no hope of replenishment. This drives people mad. Reacting in angered aggression toward each other, they roar in vicious contempt when immersed in traffic, in frustration searching for blame, any opportunity for blame, and flip profane gestures like a form of hello.

People are bound and gagged everywhere, deprived of all their personal freedom, left flopping in frustration. You can walk into a store and find someone screaming at another person that he or she doesn't even know, about the cost of something that person didn't even make, thinking it is going to make a difference in the sale.

People have to be so right about things that don't even matter. They're desperate to maintain at least some control, some sense of domination over anything that can provide opportunity to prove their personal point of righteousness. This is the context in which they choose to define freedom and power, choking all hope of any real self-expression, and consistently and inevitably, they are left desperate and defeated, ranting and raging.

I think of the many deals we have done through BPI and business deals in general, and what the world would be like if we could actually eliminate the whole concept of domination. What if our entire existence could simply be rooted in acceptance and self-expression?

The thing is, the people who are dominating are the same ones that you'll find in an elevator who feel such a terrible panicked intrusion of personal space that they stand like frightened little mice, backed into their respective corners, incapable of eye contact, let alone of initiating conversation. Insecure and frustrated with no place for accusation, fearful that they may, in fact, be held responsible for anything they do say, they stand only to stare anxious and uncomfortable at the slow-moving lights and pray for escape. Skirting the eyes of others, they allow judgment to play over and over in their minds, feeling that this is how to maintain their own level of superiority.

"What is it about relationships that is so fearful? Are loneliness, isolation and depression not big enough deterrents?" Jasmine questions. "People can't see that their fear of accepting each part of themselves is causing their own alienation," she states.

I listen to her and know that I, too—after being such a short time ago in my own personal breakdown with Julian—have been spending so much of my own energy fighting the very experience I actually wanted to create. This is what is causing the struggle. What would actually be possible in life if I could simply turn to accept all aspects of myself without resistance? I sit and wonder. What would be possible for a planet full of people who could do the same? Could we just stop the fighting, the negative behaviour, and simply move through it and beyond?

"So, that's where I was and I didn't want to be driven by something I didn't believe in anymore," Jasmine confesses with conviction.

"I wanted more than a shell of a life; I wanted a real one. And I was ready to do the work. It's the work that matters," she declares.

Jasmine believes that if you don't possess the undying desire to uncover your mind and soul, to dig deep within yourself, you are as useful as whole espresso beans without a grinder. You may well possess the sultriest of all worldly taste, with depth and full-bodied aroma, but if there is no hope of releasing your flavour for consumption, there is no point in creating a space for your useless supply.

I am motivated by her thinking and want to find a way to break through myself, to reveal and to release. I want the return of a pulse-racing life, where I can bounce out of bed, ready to take it all on. I want to feel the vibration of blood racing through my veins. I want the excitement, the search and the wonder of what great, new adventure could possibly be next.

"Dos por uno. Por dos mis amors," the bartender returns and teasingly announces as he brings us the second half of our two-for-one cocktails.

Jasmine and I enjoy the remainder of the afternoon by the pool as she shifts from the stories that once held her from her life,to those that now inspire her daily as a local.

∞∞∞∞∞∞∞∞

BANG. BANG. BANG. I awake the next morning to what I think is a loud knock at my door, only to realize the pounding is coming from outside, where I see a man suspended and swinging from the electrical pole in front of my window.

"Cab-lay," he enunciates loudly and slowly for me with a big smile, nodding his head up and down as he watches me entering the kitchen.

A thousand and one ways how to kill yourself in Mexico, is all I can think as I watch him swing from the pole that has at least a dozen thick, black wires hanging from it and wonder to what, if anything, he is actually even attached.

"No problema," I reply quietly and in slow syllables, realizing I am now officially engaged in a conversation with a strange man who is hanging from what, I hope, is at least a cable of some kind and looking into my window.

"Por su tele," he hollers back and smiles broadly with both his eyes and mouth open as wide as possible.

"Gracias," I respond with a small, forced acknowledgement.

Ah, yes, my television, and an absolute priority for me over sleep right now, I think sarcastically, as I am immediately reminded of that pessimistic, self-righteous reflex Jasmine and I had been so carefully identifying yesterday. In all honesty, I am sure this was only a humble man attempting to do his job well and actually believing he was providing me with a great service.

"No problema, muchas gracias," I say again, attempting to make up for my mute and unjustified sarcasm.

I pull the decorative coffee tin and Bodum from the back of the kitchen counter, lifting the lid off of each container and scooping four heaping spoons of the medium-roasted Mexican grounds into the glass French press. Igniting the gas stove, I stand by the window and wait for the water to heat, to make some fresh coffee for myself.

"*Useful as whole espresso beans without a grinder . . .*" is what Jasmine had said. I hum to myself in contemplation and wonder if I could dig that deep and, if so, am I really capable of complete release?

Looking out over the back patio, I notice there has already been a heavy shower this morning, but all seems to be rapidly heating to the day's expected mugginess. It is the beginning of the rainy season here; these short and torrential showers will be the norm for the next few months, Jasmine explained yesterday.

Once my coffee is ready, I take a full mug and a towel with me outside to wipe off a seat on the patio and sit to overlook the ocean and organize my day in my mind. I have decided I will take Jasmine's advice and pack a bag for the beach today. She is right: I could use some quiet time to think on what my own needs might be right now, if nothing else. We are meeting for breakfast at 10:00 a.m. at a restaurant on North Beach. I head back into the house to get ready.

∞∞∞∞∞∞∞∞

The taxi drops me off in the middle of the downtown core. I slowly saunter along the main street in the centre of town, passing the local shops, watching their owners now opening for the day. Although definitely not in much of a shopping mood, I find myself lured by the invitation of one particular shopkeeper on my way to the restaurant, who convinces me to come in and view his store. Not entirely sure of what has actually hooked me, I still do find myself entering to linger over his array of fine sculptures and various pieces of silver and, surprisingly, notice myself rather entertained by his suggestive banter.

After several minutes of mindless browsing, I thank him and move on.

Once at the restaurant, I settle at a table next to the ocean and wait for Jasmine, thinking back again to our conversations from yesterday when she admitted to me that she had not always been such a happy and well-balanced person. Recalling her story about when she finally made her break and left Chicago, I try to imagine Jasmine as an angry woman.

∞∞∞∞∞∞∞∞

"Do you have any idea what caused your injury?" the store clerk at her local health food store had innocently inquired.

Idea? Of course she did, but could this woman handle the truth, Jasmine questioned. How could she explain that she had been violated by no outside force? How could she tell this woman she had inflicted this excruciating pain on herself?

Jasmine contemplated her story.

"I was driving home from the party I was at with this idiot who, at this point in my pathetic life, I call my boyfriend. I was so angry that I have, once again, allowed myself to be mentally tormented to the extent I have. I am so unhappy with my career and my inability to pinpoint even the slightest desire of what I need in life, let alone what I want to do. And I am too weak to allow the expression of my own voice for fear of being excluded by those who do not even know I exist. So I screamed. I screamed in absolute and utter agony. I screamed so loud and so long that I couldn't speak this morning and only recently have I been, once again, blessed with speech. In fact, I believe that scream has either severely ruptured my throat, causing this intolerable pain or some demented physician crawled into my bed last night and fed a long, thin instrument through my gaping mouth and scraped the back of my throat until it bled, which I might add, is very, highly unlikely. Regardless, I need some fucking comfort and I need it NOW!"

Instead of saying any of this, she remained calm, maintained her composure, blinked her eyes innocently at the woman who had absolutely no idea what the world was truly about and simply uttered, "I'm not really sure." She mustered the only meagre smile of which she was capable. Then she shrugged her shoulders lightly and answered in a whisper, "Perhaps, I'm getting that cold that seems to be going around."

"Lot of people are," the clerk empathized. "I have just the thing."

Inundated by outsiders' suggestions as to what she should do and what she should feel, she felt nothing, nothing but aggravation. Living in a desperate world, she continually found herself caught doing the same thing repeatedly, to no avail. The pain she had brought upon herself was simply to let herself know that she was still capable of feeling, feeling anything beyond the deafening numbness that was consuming her life. That night Jasmine had screamed for every woman who had ever betrayed herself.

 The next morning she left Chicago.

∞∞∞∞∞∞∞∞

I take a sip of my coffee. The shouting and endless chatter inside my own mind is waning. I have not miraculously stumbled on any answers to my own lifelong running questions, but the judging, the incessant analyzing, seems to be winding down for the moment. The music in the background calms my mind, allowing me to look deeper.

 I fight to maintain a balance for myself, struggling to really understand what it means. My normal reaction is simply to shut down, carry on, ensure all goes as planned—no ripples, no bumps and, certainly, no honest declarations. This harbours a death inside of me, not unlike the one Jasmine so aptly described last night, whereby I am repeatedly performing the same fruitless action and producing the exact unchanged result. And, like any habit, the more I have continued in the same, routinized behaviour, the more efficient I have become, until my life no longer requires any conscious effort at all. I wonder if there will ever be a way back for me, to the stillness, to the happiness, to the normalcy of living. Jasmine explained last night how life was for her at that time.

"Inside I was bankrupt, with no hope at all. I put hours into destroying myself, sabotaging anything that even hinted at a moment of satisfaction or gave off a whiff of success. All that fighting, and all I had to do was deal with my feelings. Instead, I was constantly filling, patching, fixing, changing. Nothing worked. As much as I tried to let go, I only recreated the same self-sabotaging world for myself every day. And why? No idea, really. My underlying commitment seemed to be insanity. Looking objectively, it's not what I would choose for myself, but I'd never been a logical person. I lived my life by the heart, not the mind, and not many people can relate. This left me tormented with justifications, explanations, trying to fit into a life I didn't even want. Why do people need a reason to do something? And why do they need to understand mine?" she questioned.

No matter how much Jasmine tried to change herself nothing altered, and she always found herself back at the same starting point, only to repeat the process over again in a more severe state to prove herself wrong. Her story is very similar to my dream and, perhaps, closer than I am even willing to realize to my own life.

"When you're desperate for change, Natalie, you're so overwhelmed, even the moment of beginning is useless," Jasmine observed. "Everything gets to the point where it's absolutely hopeless, utter despair, but you start anyway. Because you know there's something, somewhere. There has to be. You don't know how, but you know it's there. You know there's something bigger than you. Then change happens, on a dime. All the time you spend procrastinating, justifying, complaining and ignoring, and all you really need to do is just make the change. It takes one minute. The problem is choosing the moment. People think the moment needs to come with inspiration, but your time comes when you choose your moment."

Her words ring through my head. She simply changed her mind and designed a whole new life for herself. I am envious of her courage. I begin to question my own intentions and think about all the advice Eman has given me around creating my thoughts and my life with intent. Perhaps they are both right. All I need now is another moment.

As I watched Jasmine last night, I began to see success in a different light, realizing I have worked my entire life to be successful and actually hold no idea of what this even looks like. And yet I still choose to live this driven life with the expectation of getting there. No matter how many contracts I could accumulate for BPI, it was becoming increasingly clearer to me that if I didn't start outlining a real definition of success for myself, acquiring it was going to be impossible. I have accumulated many things in my life, but because I have neglected to specifically state what I truly desire, not one has granted me any real fulfillment. Despite all the things I have done and all the places I have been, I am beginning to realize, I am a failure in my own eyes. I am controlled by fear, fear of saying what I truly want and fear of actually getting everything I have ever imagined. I reflect back again to the conversation I had with Marco on my last trip to the Caribbean and realize that I, too, talk a lot and say nothing.

"Many thought I was running away. I wasn't. I found my life here," Jasmine admitted.

Jasmine allowed herself the freedom to create her own life and gave up being controlled by what others might think or say. She felt that the world was infested by the meaning of it all, the truth, the message, as if it existed out there as some reality and decided her life wasn't going to be lived by another's interpretation. And I had to agree: people are obsessed. You can see it anywhere you look—on billboards, in newspapers, on the faces of your next door neighbours and in the wrinkles they accumulate over the years. Hell, if you look close enough, you can see it happen in a week.

Meaning has inundated the planet like a god, a fourth seat in the Holy Trinity. And no matter how much promotion the Father, Son and Holy Ghost can muster, even with the advantage of a long history, meaning rules with unanimous dictatorship. It possesses children as early as their first word with *Why?* being the initial and incessant question from their tongues, a question that will never be answered. It's the drug of the century. Everything stands for something. There's a food or an herb or a fix or an app for everything. It's the name of the game, and people spend their life trying to figure it all out. One has to believe, and if you don't, you had better have a greater alternative and know how that means something more than what the masses are buying into.

"What does it matter? What if there's nothing to figure out?" Jasmine questioned.

As much as I could sit back and condemn others and their idiocy in the search of it all, I have followed in the same pursuit like a heathen sheep, whereby meaning is to me as grass is to an animal. I need it, and without it, I, too, would be unable to survive. I am an addict, just like the rest of the world.

"Freedom's the universal objective, is it not?" Jasmine continued in her inquiry. "To be free, to be exactly who we want, without judgment or distraction, without fear or obligation. What did we need a global knife at our throats for, screaming, 'Have the life you want or you, my friend, are a dead man!'? Don't we have that already? What are we all so afraid of—living? After all, what do we do beyond the struggle? We act as if the struggle is essential for most of us, but is it?" she rhetorically asked, before directing her questions to me.

"If you could release all that was deemed as a problem in your life, to be entirely freed from any blockage, to enjoy success and fulfillment, then what? Could you ever truly let go of everything that's familiar to you? Can you not remember the ache of anxiety in your stomach just before your first kiss or the energy of a young, hot sweating palm on your inner thigh, wanting each inch of something new? God, I remember Jimmie Thompson like it was yesterday—dirty dancing to some raunchy beat in the backyard, while food burned on the barbeque, and the only thing we really cared about was making out on the lawn in broad daylight. Nothing else mattered."

And she was right. I, too, had allowed the age of innocence, when monotony was never even an option, to slip away. Jasmine took it back. She lived in a world where each second existed as a new minute of possibility, where power was in freedom, not money.

I have preached this life but never had the courage to actually live it. The door has opened several times for me, but I never seem to walk through. This stubbornness allows for a certain amount of success, as stubbornness can, but I know I am limited. My inability to accept life, as it is, holds me back from its true experience.

In our talks yesterday, I saw something for myself I have refused to acknowledge before now. My stubbornness is my responsibility. I haven't been owning it as mine. I've been denying it, resisting it, even being right about it, but I certainly haven't been accepting any of it as part of who I actually am.

No, in my world, I have taken all the right steps: the education, the career, the lifestyle to progress, but what I am beginning to see now is that it is my own resignation and resistance that is continually propelling me like a ship with no captain, aimlessly and constantly thrusting me into oceans of upheaval. I claim a quest of mastery and look like I am out there swashbuckling and commanding, knee-deep and full of adventure, yet I cannot move my mind beyond simply managing the chaos. I am a pirate, and the only act of violence being committed is war on myself. I am robbing myself of the only life I have ever wanted, working viciously to create it and then unconsciously throwing it all overboard. For such an educated and forward-thinking person, I am beginning to realize that I really am quite dumb.

 I squeeze my eyes tightly before looking back at the ocean, calm and serene. I have tried throughout my life to be careful and in control of all that has fallen within my path. What do I have? A place on the hill with a beautiful view, a career and a home in the country, where I can avoid everyone and everything. What is this obsessive need for control really all about?

 It is the anniversary of their deaths today, Brendan and my mother. I miss them, terribly. I have convinced myself I am doing what I want in life; in actuality, I know I have carved an entire existence that means nothing, a place where I live safely and untouched. I spend my life avoiding and prohibiting myself any freedom to feel or to expand. Based on the past few weeks of getting to know Jasmine, and on our time together yesterday, I have a hunch that she is going to blow this protected little existence of mine wide open.

∞∞∞∞∞∞∞

"Hola, Ms. Natalie," Jasmine sings as she enters.

The waiter pulls her chair from the table and kisses the side of her cheek. "Buenos," he acknowledges.

"Buenos. Gracias, senor," she whispers with a sweet softness as the waiter smiles and lightly blushes.

Jasmine has a subtle but direct approach about her that is almost uncomfortable. She reaches inside and lingers just a little too long, making you feel special or fearful of what you think she actually might see. This seductive demeanour is extremely intoxicating, digging deep and leaving you with the feeling that she really does understand you. As dangerous as it might be for each individual, all are left wanting her attention even though she might uncover something forbidden or unappreciated that may have been entirely neglected before now. I am not sure what you call this type of person—a mystic, a psychologist, a lawyer or a saint. I suppose it depends on the depth of one's fear of being found.

"Hola, Jasmine," I respond.

"And how are you this morning, Ms. Natalie?" She smiles with her boundless energy that sweeps in and lifts any remaining heaviness from the morning.

"Ready for balance," I admit, smirking back at her.

"Great. So, how did I meet her?" Jasmine acknowledges and then immediately starts, as if answering a question I have already asked.

"When I first came to the island, I got a job at a small café right in the centre of town. I worked the breakfast shift each morning. One morning in particular, I was telling my girlfriend what had happened the day before, how I had been robbed at the beach.

"'They weren't locales. Inland, I think. Just up for the day. Two of the guys asked me a lot of questions about the island. While I was talking to them, the other younger two obviously rifled through my bag. I had no idea. I even waved goodbye to them. When I left, they were sitting at the bar with at least a dozen Coronas in front of them. Cervezas I had obviously paid for. Never realized till later that night, when I went to the supermarket and found my wallet empty.'

"'You're kidding, no way,' my girlfriend replied.

"Karina had her back to us, but spoke loud enough for both of us to hear her: 'If you learn to depend on yourself, you take the first step into the real world. If you can trust yourself, you may survive,' she said, holding her coffee cup to her lips with both hands, before taking a slow sip and placing it back down on the table in front of her.

"Looking straight out the doorway onto the street and never actually directly at us, she continued, 'Actually, believin' will be your biggest step. Ya gotta keep the faith.'

"The interaction seemed strange at the time but started a string of conversations between the two of us. She came in every day after that and I would serve her, and we would talk. Her insight helped me through a lot that first year. Well, the dancer is a story about her, her story."

"I'd like to speak with her. Is she still living on the island?"

"Nope, died a little over a year ago."

"Oh, I'm sorry."

"Si, my poor Karina," Jasmine whispers with distant eyes.

"What about the lover you mentioned?" I say softly, respecting her loss.

"Very wealthy. His family didn't approve of Karina. Against his parents' approval, they still managed to find a way to see each other. Karina became pregnant. The family got heated, investigated her lineage and discovered she was from a long line of gypsies. Her grandmother was actually a real gypsy. Well, completely unacceptable for the Wutherfords. After continual threats and harassment, they eventually convinced Karina she wasn't worthy of their son, Adrian. Few years later, after the baby, Adrian was away on business, and they drove her away. She didn't know what to do—no money, no family, she knew at that time—she couldn't make it on her own. So, she left, hoping at least her son could have the best life possible."

"What did Adrian say to all of this?"

"Don't think he ever really knew. From what Karina heard, they told him she moved on in the middle of the night, back to her roots, wandering."

"Unbelievable."

"She left all of her belongings to me, if you want to see them."

"Amazing," I reply stunned, trying to imagine the pain, the sacrifice that something like that would take.

"La quenta, por favor." Jasmine smiles, requesting our bill once we have finished with breakfast.

"I have to run to the market for the restaurant; hear they have some fresh romaine today," she acknowledges in excitement, closing her eyes and kissing the tips of her fingers and smacking a savoury kiss into mid-air.

Smiling back at me again and shrugging her shoulders in delight, she continues.

"Want to meet up a little later?"

"Sure. I'd like to go to the church today."

"Ah, the tequila. Makes us all ask for forgiveness," she consoles and smirks.

"Yes." I smile. "Actually, I would like to go and light a candle."

"Sure. Listen, if you want to come with me to the market, we'll drop off the supplies at the restaurant and I'll go with you. I always like to light a candle for Ms. Karina," she whispers in adoration.

"Perfect."

I pay the bill, and we set out for the market.

NINE

Let nothing disturb you, nothing dismay you. All things are passing, God never changes. Patient endurance attains all things...God suffices.

—Saint Teresa of Avila

Harmonic and angelic voices elevate to chilling levels as we solemnly walk up the cement steps into the church in the centro. A single soprano voice reaches above the rest and is soon followed by the accompanying chorus. I have come to pay my private tribute, and although alone in my individual grief, I do feel as if I am part of a grander union, something much larger than myself. Slowly, we enter through the crowd. Faces, unknown and many sheltered by their ritualistic cloth and garment, create a sea of anonymity where vanity plays no role, passes no judgment. I am amongst acceptance. There are no whispers. I am undefined, lost in the mass of this chanting room, yet I feel such a connection to the whole, and to these people I have never met. I feel at home, accepted in this cathedral I have not entered, before now.

∞∞∞∞∞∞

It had been the opposite the day Brendan and my mother were buried. Standing at the foot of the two mahogany boxes, beside my father at the church, all I could hear were whispers—*How is she doing? That poor girl.*—each telling me what I should do, what I should wear, how I must be strong in times like these. My mother was dead. She would not be noticing my clothes today. In fact, this was never of any importance to her. Her love was not conditional and it certainly was not based on my brand of clothing. They would have no understanding of that. I gave them nothing.

In an entire room of familiar faces, I felt alone and empty. I did not shed a single tear. I held every remaining one tight in my body, in a reservoir for myself. I merely stood as smothering hands hovered over me and attempted to squeeze their way into my space. I wanted to scream; I wanted them back. I stood, instead, with blank eyes for what seemed like days and perfected my reality, until I could no longer feel at all. That day, everyone wanted something, and I decided, in that moment, no one would ever, ever have anything again. And as for God, he had taken all he was ever going to get.

I performed and later left, keeping each emotion buried deep within me, from that moment on. I realize now, it was that one single second of not being able to accept love for myself that changed my entire life. I spent the next three decades punishing myself for that one moment I was unable to love and unwilling to be comforted by those who were still living. Looking back now, however, it's easy to see that when we make these crucial decisions in life, we are not aware at the time, but there is no escape from the fate. Our life will eventually become centred around these exact beliefs, attracting all that is required to prove our story just, until the actual truth will eventually not even be required to play any part at all. Another failed relationship for me, once again, proved this theory.

Until we can see these beliefs for what they are, we are bound by their lies, strangled and suffocated by their story. Only when we can finally look from a place outside of our own limitations can we see an alternative perspective and find hope.

∞∞∞∞∞∞∞∞

Now standing in this crowd of unknown faces, I begin to accept a sense of freedom for myself and, perhaps, even a slight forgiveness. I breathe deeply and begin to experience a small feeling of revival and, finally, a certain sense of release of things I have carried for far too long—the same ones I actually never had any ability to control in the first place.

Intuitively, I walk through the crowd, trusting and allowing myself to believe that this, too, shall pass. All gently sway to clear a path for me, and I feel like I am a child again, cradled and attended to the way I wanted to be the day my mother and brother died.

Jasmine explains that today is Memorial Day, honouring St. Teresa of Avila, a renowned saint and mystic born in 16th-century Spain, in a time when the voice of a woman was deemed to be of little importance. I find her story surprisingly similar to my own and her journey incredibly inspiring. With the death of her mother at the age of fourteen, her father had arranged for her education in a local convent. I can relate, although I had been sent away before my mother died, and was much younger. As St. Teresa realized at that time, she had accepted her destiny of being sent away due more to fear rather than to her own devotion to God or the church. It was not until much later, when she began to loathe the mediocrity of her own spirituality, that she came to devote herself more seriously.

Despite the societal shortcomings of her time, she studied to become a well-accomplished writer, authored four books and founded seventeen convents. St. Teresa believed the soul was a castle made of a single diamond. She was convinced everyone had only one soul and one life, which was short and to be lived by each individually. She felt that if a person could remember these simple concepts, there would be many things that would appear meaningless in light of the person's grander purpose. I am not as spiritual as a renowned nun, but I can understand this. What I still struggle to see at this time, however, is what that larger purpose is for me.

I feel strangely connected to this woman, being the saint honoured on the exact day Brendan and my mother died. We enter a small prayer room to the left, where a picture of St. Teresa hangs on the concrete wall, encased in glass. A thin blue border outlines the habit that trails down each side of her face, while the rest remains white. I step closer and stare directly into her eyes, seeing my own reflection in the glass. Does it matter she's dead? That was the job of a saint, was it not, to support patrons indefinitely? I think of all the things I still harbour and how they mean nothing to the overall view of my life yet have so easily come to define it. For a moment, I sit back and feel this incredible overwhelming wave of bottomless remorse for all the time that has been lost, for which I must now learn to make up.

We walk back to the main room, light a large wooden match and bend to ignite the candle along the front altar. Leaning forward and kneeling to bow my head, I notice a spider web in the corner underneath the wood. Immediately, I think of gooseberries and the time Brendan and I picked them from the forbidden bush. Even as a young child, I thought this had been our justifiable punishment. We were not supposed to eat the berries and we deserved the dreaded taste of their dusty soil and tart fruit, for we had sinned, my father's sister had preached. We deserved our afternoon of wretched vomiting as punishment. We should have known better and done as we were told.

Bad things happen to bad people. We were bad people. My mother had not agreed when we later returned home and she had words with my father after dinner, only moments after Brendan questioned who Satan was. We did not have to go there again for a long time.

There was nothing we could have done to deserve our fate. If only I could have known a hint of the future, I would have never allowed my father to send me away. I would have found a way, somehow. So much had been taken for granted, if only we'd had more time. So many nights of aching, waiting to see them, and in one short breath they were gone, gone forever. I would never see them again.

∞∞∞∞∞∞∞

"You're not looking hard enough. They're there," I screamed at my father that night as he quietly tried to explain what happened, while on the other end of the phone.

"There's been a terrible accident, Natalie."

"NOOO!!!! They're there; you're not looking hard enough. They're *THERE,*" I angrily insisted through clenched teeth.

I called my father a liar.

They were there. He was wrong.

"On the water; the boat collapsed."

The nun took the telephone from my hand as I ran down the arched hallway and out the front doors. I ran into the courtyard and hid. I ran to build a world where they still existed for me.

Adorning me with seaweed treasures, they swim to me in my dream. No one can take them from me. I can see the sun shining through the crystal water as they approach.

They are not gone. They are here with me. I knew I could find them.

We play in the water, swimming circles, flipping up into the air and down to the depths of the ocean floor. We swim around the rock, sitting so rigid and unwilling to bend. We play games, trying to impress him with the wiggle of our tails and our bright yellow fins. The water is our friend and is taking us to places far unknown, together. We will move on to wonderful new levels, but the rock will linger in anger. No longer will we waste our beautiful energy on him. Our brilliance will shine amidst the deepest parts of the ocean and together we will no longer try to change his rigid life. We will not allow for division. United, we will move on to provide others with a way to see the true light, the true meaning, the true blue. Happiness will be our destination, and the water will set us free.

The nuns found me in the morning still sleeping quietly under the big oak in the garden.

∞∞∞∞∞∞

Jasmine touches my shoulder, and we both rise and leave. Outside the cathedral, an old woman stands beside a white-cloaked table, selling small trinkets of various religious memorabilia in front of the plaza. As we make our way to pass her, she gently touches my arm and pulls me toward her. I stop as Jasmine continues walking through the square. The woman holds me tighter now, in front of her and rubs my arms quickly up and down. Her body is round and worn. Her face is leathery and old. I smile, looking into her drooping, dark brown eyes that are lined with a slight red tinge and attempt to pull away, but she refuses to let go.

She places the palms of her hands on my face and keeps repeating something over and over again in Spanish. I cannot understand her. She pulls my face toward her and kisses both sides and then directs me toward her trinket collection, fondling over the plastic cards lying there, while still securely holding my arm.

"No, no, no," she mutters repeatedly and very quickly under her breath. "Si, si, si, si," she continues to herself as her hand hovers over the arrangement, like a grand magician about to grant me my future.

She selects two cards, each with coloured photos on the front and scripted text on the back and wraps them both in small plastic baggies and tucks them in the front of my shirt pocket.

"Si, si, si," she confirms and pats my pocket, shaking her head affirmatively.

Standing before me, she takes my hands with both of hers and turns them over and then bends down to kiss the centre of both my palms. Standing upright to face me once again, she smiles and slowly reaffirms, "Si . . . si . . . si."

I ask her how much, at this point thinking that the only way I will get away from her is to buy these items. She shakes her head and lightly blinks her eyes, no. I accept whatever she is giving me and turn and finally walk away, wondering what exactly has just taken place.

"What was that about?" I question Jasmine, once I catch up with her.

"A blessing," Jasmine replies.

I am uncertain if she is referring to my lack of understanding of what has just taken place or the actual gift.

∞∞∞∞∞∞∞∞

Later in the afternoon, I take a long walk by myself into the *colonias*. Separated from the mainstream core, on the other side of the island is the locale part of town, the real life of the island. Unlike the tourist centre, parts of it are very poor. I go farther along the road, passing the *tortilleria*, and see the ladies busy in their production of the island's daily batch of tortillas. Donning their large white caps and standing in their multi-coloured patterned shorts with large white aprons and big pockets that fall mid-calf, they stand to bake the sustenance for the island. Piling their finished products in neat stacks, they package the warmth of soft tortillas within papered lining. Their task is simple, yet these women work proudly, unaffected by any monotony. It is not about what they are doing here, but who they are for each other. I watch them as they laugh and joke. Their job is not about money or position. They have a purpose together. This bakery provides the staple for this entire place and all of its visitors. Its production cannot be achieved successfully single-handedly. I begin to see the definition of duty in a way I have never seen before now. They are the pillars of their community, each holding a very important job, and together they make a huge difference for this place.

A young man stands out front, packing the picnic cooler he has strapped to the back of his bicycle with the packets of warm tortillas that he will soon deliver throughout the neighbourhood. With the squeak of his bike horn he travels from street to street, delivering the fresh tortillas straight to the front door of those who step out and signal him. Home delivery is a common convenience out here, I notice as I watch the big trucks delivering *garrafóns* of water and propane tanks, and many large tricycles and other vendors selling their various vegetables, baked goods and fresh cheeses. I listen to the distinctive advertising chants as they sing their own unique songs through the streets, announcing today's menu of homemade tamales, *elotes* and *crème de la coco*. I stop to buy some fresh handmade cheese from Oaxaca from a barefooted man dressed all in white, who carries his dairy-filled cardboard box balanced perfectly on his head. His voice is of a strong, operatic nature and one that carries clearly through several streets as he sings in long, even intervals.

"KAAAAY . . . SOOOO . . . WA-HAWK-KA."

Singing the words *Queso Oaxaca*, he announces the arrival of his fresh cheese for sale. Queso Oaxaca, I am about to learn, is delicious long ribbons of white curd-like cheese wound into a large ball and sliced in various sizes. The man smiles and cuts me a healthy-sized triangle as I hand him my pesos and peel a big string of its warm, moist rubber, which is soft and silky and tastes slightly salty. Quickly, I rewrap my new purchase and hide it deep in the bottom of my bag, knowing if I don't put it away now, my tasty new discovery is never going to make it home.

After walking for the better part of the afternoon, I stop at a sign that reads "Cold drink" on its cardboard surface. I enter through the interlocking vines at the front entrance and proceed to the back of the house, where a lady sits in front of a small cooler.

"Hola! Coca?" she questions.

"Aqua?" I ask politely.

"Coca Lite?" she responds, obviously answering my question.

"Si, por favor," I agree and hand her my pesos.

She counts the coins, drops them into the front of her dress and then hands me two pesos in return.

"Ocho," she announces.

"No, no, por favor," I respond smiling, leaving the extra two pesos with her as I accept my drink and take a seat on a small crate beside a thin, unstable piece of plywood that rests on some old, plastic milk crates. The area is cluttered and lined in books. There must be at least a hundred, some in different languages: Spanish, German, English, Italian and French. I look at the woman, who does not seem greatly affected by my presence.

"Do you read all of these books?" I ask her in Spanish, wishing I knew the language better than I did.

"Si," she answers, crossing her brows in clear affirmation and then smiles.

I am not sure she has understood what I have said. Standing, she turns, lifts a small curtain and enters another part of the house, leaving me by myself.

My hands are swollen from the walk. The air is humid and hot. I knew it would be. I just had never imagined how much it really could be. I remove my ring and allow it to rock upon the uneven table, clutching the cold glass bottle in an attempt to reduce the swelling. My ring . . . reminds me of my mother and when I used to play with her in the garden in the mornings when I was young.

∞∞∞∞∞∞∞∞

Wearing her ring, I would pretend I was the mother. With a scarf around my head, I would dance with tilted hand before me and sing to her. She would laugh as I fluttered about, swiping the silk scarf across her peach-coloured skin and prancing in circles around the yard. I loved to hear her laugh and always did whatever it took. King of the castle, I would play and jump upon my wagon, shouting victory, only to bow and transform myself into a beautiful ballet dancer, twirling in circles. Those times when it was just the two of us, I did not exist, except as the chameleon that provided her with joy.

∞∞∞∞∞∞∞∞

I take a long sip of my drink, then set the bottle on the table and pull a book from the shelf. Opening to the scent of attic-stored, yellowed pages, I lift the inside cover to find someone's faded handwritten thoughts.

> Possession, ownership ~ true control can never be gained if one does not first possess the mind that leads the action.
> Belonging ~ to feel attachment, to be part of an entity. To be part of an entity, one must first understand the feeling that coincides with unity. If one has no definition of unity, one is incapable of feeling.
> Intimacy ~ to reach beyond the intensity of emotion to experience closeness, innocence, the ability to be vulnerable, to feel beyond the self, to develop deep affection.
> Love ~ utter adoration and respect without condition, without question, without fear.
> Vacancy ~ the state to which one retreats for fear of all of these things, empty of emotion for fear of depletion, denial, disrespect, misunderstanding, restriction and regression. Vacancy ~ to feel nothing.

I sit now and wonder about my mother's definition of unity. She would rather sit alone in her mind. Her pain, her suffering, was greater than any love she would ever desire. She was only truly content in being with herself. Her mind allowed for a certain serenity, carrying her away to exciting corners without threat. She forced herself to socialize at times, justifying her endeavours as opportunity to understand human behaviour. She had no intention of being seduced into a mindless world that was common, a world in which she did not want to belong. Few understood her. I am reminded of the woman at the church.

I set my empty bottle neatly in the plastic crate near the door and make my way back to the beach house, thinking now only of the last line I have just read.

Vacancy ~ to feel nothing.

∞∞∞∞∞∞∞∞

My heels are raw from my afternoon adventure. As much as I tried, I was unable to remove the tiny grains of sand that kept sneaking under the straps of my sandals. Once accustomed to the pain, I finally gave up trying and let the thin layer of perspiration win to create two very sizable blisters on the back of my heels. As I sit now at dinner with Jasmine and rest my feet on the edge of my sandals, I am reminded, even the smallest grain left unacknowledged will fester and cause debilitating pain.

"How did you begin writing?" I ask Jasmine.

"Always wrote, stories in my head, just never wrote it down."

The server places a basket of warm flour tortillas on our table. I smile, now knowing their origin, reminded of the ladies from this afternoon and nurtured by a sense of close community.

Jasmine reaches to her left, to the old wooden Mexican cabinet near the table, and grabs a pear from the arrangement of decorative fruit sitting there.

"This is what made me finally write."

"How's that?" I question, intrigued by the possible connection.

"Karina's strength had been dwindling for quite some time. About two weeks before she died, I went over to her house to make her dinner. She was sitting at the table eating a pear. Her movements were slow. I arranged the plates on the table, watching her from the corner of my eye. I saw her very gently begin to reach for my hand. I set the plate down and sat next to her.

"She smiled and studied my face for quite some time and then, emphasizing each word, slowly said, 'This is a really good pear.'

"She exaggerated like it was a secret code, as if I was to know what it meant. I knew she was sick, but her mind was still sharp. She was not talking about the fruit."

Jasmine twirls the plastic pear between us and continues. "She was telling me something, but I didn't know what she was saying. She believed that if a person was to truly understand a lesson, she needed to find the answer herself. She was telling me the message of the lesson I needed to learn. Her eyes travelled through me. I stared so intensely at her I saw nothing else. Her eyes had a way of cradling, protecting, guiding, almost as if her arms were around you. I knew from her look that it was important I understand her.

"She often said, 'The simplest things give us the greatest pleasures.'"

"Perhaps that is what she was telling you in her description of the pear," I offer.

"Yeah, like remembering the little things, maybe, but, it was more than that. Never in her own life had she taken anything for granted. She was a woman who did nothing but give to those around her. She spent her life sharing everything she had. As I watched her, I saw there was no one to share her pain. She alone had to bear the biggest burden of all. I could sit with her, but there was nothing I could do to stop the pain.

"Looking at her depleted body, I began to realize the cruelty of life. She didn't deserve it. I could do nothing to change her reality. I held her hand, realizing for the first time that I was afraid for her to die. I didn't want to be without her. Her skin was frail. I patted her hand and thought of the many times it had saved me throughout our friendship. Karina leaned forward and kissed the side of my cheek.

"'Thanks for coming, Jas,' she whispered into the skin on my face. I felt the heat of her breath and her face against mine and closed my eyes as a tear dripped down the side of my face. I knew the day was coming and I didn't want to let go. I knew the volcanoes of pain that were increasingly erupting inside of her were going to win and I wanted them to stop.

"'I wouldn't be anywhere else,' I said, attempting to be strong, almost embarrassed at her strength and my lack of it. I watched her leg shake uncontrollably beneath the table and placed my hand on her knee to slow her tremble.

"What I discovered later, through some further research, is that the pear is believed to be the seed of new beginnings and is thought to hold the secrets of life and death. Karina had come full circle. What I discovered is that eating the pear feeds the deep creative hunger to write and provides ways to put forward hopes and ideas and creations in a way the world has never seen before. Realizing this, I knew I had to take charge and ensure everyone noticed the flavour of the pear. It was the one gift I could give Karina. There was nothing else for me to do, but write her story."

We sit in silence for a few moments. Jasmine and I stare into each other's eyes and share the pain. Tonight we are celebrating mutual losses, forbidden fruits and the strength it takes to be true to yourself. We lift our glasses and toast to all that has been wrongfully taken and to all that will soon be reclaimed with our project. I begin to see an entirely new definition of responsibility arising, something completely outside of myself and, yet, something very deep within. And I am starting to firmly believe that this story is the purpose, the one for which I have been endlessly searching. I can feel it.

I came to this island to get the story, to land the client and make the deal. This woman now sitting across from me, a waitress on a small island in the Caribbean, is now changing everything I have ever known to be true about people, and myself. The life I had a few weeks ago seems far away, and my cynical edge is further eroding with each conversation. Jasmine is altering my entire view and making it all personal. Listening to her is stopping me from the destruction, the continuous game of acquisition and delivery that I have constructed as my entire way of being and getting what I want in the world. Her stories are making me aware of my own life. And the blatant reality is that I have nothing at stake for myself, no real purpose, no grander plan. I have all carefully and methodically arranged so I can predict each action and every result yet have nothing that makes me want to race to life's limits. I have come a long way to find answers to my questions and I am realizing, more and more, that I am finding just the opposite.

Jasmine's clarity is allowing me to see things I have never been able to see, like the fact that I have lived my entire life thinking I have it all handled and, yet, have no sense of abundance in my life at all or even the know-how to form a good definition of what it could possibly mean. Suddenly, however, I do know I want more, and it has nothing to do with the accumulation of material objects. The more time I spend talking with Jasmine, the more I realize that I have no idea who I really am. For a moment, as I watch her and reflect on her stories of Karina, I wonder what the hell I have done with my entire life.

Hearing the celebratory clink of our glasses, the two men at the next table, whom we have not noticed until now, lean over to question our occasion. Smirking at each other, Jasmine and I both turn in their direction.

"La vida," Jasmine teases as she lifts her glass high into the air, saluting the two men and toasting life.

"Come join us," she invites.

Taking a closer look, I realize that one of the two men is Manuel, the shopkeeper I met earlier in the day.

"Gracias, senorita," the other man replies. Jasmine introduces him as Carlos when they both bring their chairs to our table.

Manuel squeezes in next to me. "I see you found your friend, senorita," he says in his low and alluring manner.

"Si, senor," I reply.

The night is wet with humidity, and the strum of a Spanish guitar sets the tone for an evening of festive activity and fun as we order another round.

"Senorita, you have tasted the food, tested the tequila, but have you danced the salsa?" Manuel demands of me.

"Oh God." I roll my eyes toward Jasmine and Carlos as they laugh.

I know there is absolutely no escape from my next cultural initiation.

"Ah, bonita, let me show you the way we dance," he insists with his undeniable tone, the same that successfully seduced me into his store earlier in the day. He extends his hand forward, holding his body in tight form, and awaits my answer. He is smooth and filled with intense vitality, and I can do nothing but accept his invitation.

Somewhat reserved at first, I soon allow Manuel to be my teacher. I have forgotten the feeling of being alive and what it feels like to dance unabashedly. Freedom is not about carving a big space to say, "I own this." It is in knowing, "I am this and I love it." Anyone can have money if they set their mind to it, but few can possess the fortune of complete richness and very few truly enjoy each moment. As I dance with Manuel, I become reconnected to this simple pleasure, realizing nothing really matters and wondering who first invented the unwinnable race and why life cannot just be one long moment like this one.

I forget about what I look like and what someone might say and put my whole self into the dancing, allowing myself to be lead by the beat and Manuel. For the moment, there are no more stories. I am open and all I can hear is the beat of the music pounding from inside my body as I trust him to lead me. I have no idea of my ability and follow his every cue, finding as I release my tight hold of control that I am granted a whole new level of living. The sweat blinks from his eyes as the music slows, and we hold each other tight. Our bodies are synchronized without any prior rehearsal—the lesson is as simple as that. If one can release the fear and simply act in the moment—without trying to control or analyze the outcome—life flows without hindrance, naturally and perfectly, no prior lesson required, no plan of attack needed, no prerequisite or pedigree.

Music is the universal road to liberation, and I am ready to be free.

This is the first time I personally begin to feel the message of Karina and the importance of the dance. She released her barriers, freed herself and danced with the full passion of life. As I look at the snuggling couples swaying to the music now, I realize I am learning the essentials of what I need to publish this book, and it sits far outside any conventional regime of interviews and contracts, clients and publishers. Whether it is Karina, Jasmine or Ixchel, someone is definitely teaching me what I need to know and the context in which I need to live passionately and free. All I know for sure is that my heart has the strangest sensation, open and lusting for life, so much so that it feels as if the excitement will consume me, and I don't care. If I had to leave this earth within the next moment, I would die a happy woman. When true desire is discovered and the soul is hungry, it will not stop at any barrier en route to its fulfillment. Without fear, there is no reason for failure. I have forgotten about the blisters on my ankles.

∞∞∞∞∞∞∞

Later in the evening, as we are about to leave, Manuel stops in the street in front of the entrance, and hugs me good night. Just as I danced with him unrestrainedly, I hold now to his friendship with the same fervour. He has opened something inside of me, and my fear is that his disappearance will take this newly discovered feeling with him. Manuel lifts his hand toward me and tilts my face slightly, gently cradling my cheek in his palm. I feel the strong warmth of his hand and both his masculinity and his softness. He looks solidly into my eyes.

"Buenos noches, senorita."

"Gracias, senor," I reply as I leave to catch a taxi back to the beach house, alone.

After walking inside and throwing my bag on the chair by the door, I get ready for bed and open the windows wide to feel the full breeze coming in from the ocean. Sprawling across the king-sized bed, I allow the wind to flutter my silk night shirt over my body. The gentle night climbs to me in a tender approach, reminding me, as Julian once did, of the woman I am. I feel the soft, smooth cotton sheets and hum to myself as my mind quiets to a restful state. I lie on my stomach and look at the water out the window and rub my hand across the bed, flattening its surface. My ring is gone. I must have left it with the woman who sold me the soft drink earlier this afternoon. I walked away and left it on the table, an option I know my mother never realized she had. I hope it would bring better fortune to the woman in the store than the countless books she had been handed, in languages she would never have the opportunity to understand.

TEN

It is never too late to become what you might have been.

—George Elliot

Morning comes quickly, and I find myself eager to start the day. The sky is pinkish with large, billowy blue-grey clouds through which the sun is about to break. The day is yet untouched by any direction, and anything seems possible. The water is an arrangement of varying degrees of violet blue and washes gently upon the shore. Moving back into the horizon, its ripples are directed by the wind that whispers in small exhalations. I stand quietly and inhale the fresh salt air. Exhaling with a deep satisfactory moan, I watch the waves roll in. They resemble hands reaching across a large sandy surface, congratulating each other on their successful journey once they reach the land.

    I twist my hair up and head out to the centro to buy some mangoes. It feels great not to worry about being perfect and pressed, and heading off to work. As I walk through the town, the morning is quiet and serene and not yet cluttered with all the tourists who will soon fill its streets. Two business owners lean in front of their shops and connect over morning coffee and a breakfast taco, both greeting me with a big "buenas dias" when I walk by.

Once inside the market, I select my mangoes for the day and wait as the old man behind the counter slowly counts out loud in Spanish as he weighs the selected items of the woman who stands in front of me. His nose is big, red and veiny, and suits him. He has a procedure for everything. Nothing hurries him. I open the plastic bag, awaiting my turn and extract a slice of the fresh-cut fruit. I swear I could live on these mangoes. Unlike home, here there are so many varieties to choose from: big, small, green, red, yellow. I am sure each holds its appropriate name and region. I only know they are absolutely mouth-watering, all of them. My turn eventually comes about and I hand the man my pesos and venture on. I pass the shops that are now beginning to open for the day, hearing the scrape of many statues being drawn to their display fronts.

"Buenos dias, salsa dancer." Manuel smiles and teases from across the street as he arranges his clay sculptures of various Mayan statues out in front of his shop.

I cross to meet him.

"Hola, como estas?"

"Muy bien y tu? I see you are picking up on your Spanish, senorita."

"Si, senor."

"You are a wild woman, Ms. Natalie."

"Manuel, you don't see me as an untamed woman, now do you?" I suggestively tease.

"Ms. Natalie, I do not need to see a thing."

I joke with him but understand the exact, unbridled energy to which he is referring. Although I allowed only a small and controlled part to surface last night, there was still a gigantic mound of desire waiting to be unleashed. I had allowed this liberation with Julian, and I was petrified to go through it all again. So, like a child at the circus door the day before opening, I got close enough to grab a peek but stood far enough away so as not to get caught, finding a perverse excitement in the world of the unknown, fighting every moment for the privilege to get there, then prohibiting myself from the full-meal deal.

The day is bright and hot, and as I venture farther down and cross over the cobblestone streets, I see a cement wall opening at the end of the road with a white, wooden gate and a large cross positioned on top of its triangular peak. In an odd location and definitely not strategically placed for tourist attraction is a graveyard, right in the centre of town. I have not noticed its existence before now but decide to walk through its opening. The entrance steps are crumbled, and the pebbles shift beneath my feet as I enter.

Once inside what seems like a desolate front, the gardens are lush and green. Huge altars are assembled in the thickness of leafy trees, with large statues and beautiful flowers adorning each monument. Unlike home, where the cemeteries are dark and precise, depressing and square, with words chiselled coldly with no sense of connection to the former individual, these are beautiful sacraments, authentically representing the people who once existed. Monuments are painted with bright colours of pink, blue and green, and gorgeous white sculptures of angels are assembled as protectors of all who lie beneath. Death here is not unfortunate, not something to be feared by those who still live. There is no barrenness, only acceptance, which is evident from the many souvenirs and fresh-cut flowers that rest upon each grave. The deceased are not forgotten but praised in recognition, routinely, if not daily. All left living continue to care for loved ones as if they are still alive. Love here is unconditional and surpasses even death, it seems.

Row by row, I walk, becoming acquainted with all those who have once resided here, noting their special interests and talents, their individual uniqueness and hobbies, which are outlined by the collections left at their grave. In my world, such recognition is hardly extended to the living, let alone the dead. I am able to learn more of the corpses that reside here than I know of the living people in my life. There is no danger here in expressing the heartfelt, for all is dealt with respectfully.

No wonder Karina chose to spend her life here, after being denied in her own environment. Here, she was not judged by the past, but adored, loved for who she was. As I think of her, I stumble upon her grave, which is not extravagant, but stately nonetheless. From what little I do know of her, her monument reflects her persona, small in stature, yet strong in presence; an absolutely undeniable aura surrounds her stone. A concrete angel stands to protect her tombstone and a medallion hangs from around its neck. Stepping closer, I lift the charm with my hand, studying its surface, and rub the face of the Black Madonna.

From what I know, renowned as the pre-historic Mother Earth and adored by the gypsies for her healing powers of transformation, the Black Madonna was the inspirational mother from the beginning of time and a woman who did not belong to any man. It is no coincidence that this medallion lies here: a symbol of wisdom and harmony, it represents one capable of resolving all conflict and hardship among rivals. She was the woman who was believed to provide life to all men. And so, too, will Karina. I will make sure of it.

I stand in honour as she lies humbly at my feet, wishing I could have known her and almost feeling as if I do. Kneeling down, I read the inscription on her stone.

> *In Lak' ech—I am you, and you are me. We are not separate. We are all part of the same, and if any part is hurt, the rest of us will suffer.*

It was the living code of the heart of the Maya and a common greeting meant to honour our unity as human beings. I have learned through my further research on the Maya that they believe everything we do affects everything else, either in a positive or negative way, depending on our actions and our intentions. If we can acknowledge and become intimately connected with the unity in life, we can positively transform the world into a place filled with love and respect. The more we can live this life, the more we can understand there is no separateness. When we give to others, we give to ourselves. We are all one.

    I sit beside her and close my eyes. I have never known vulnerability, for the exception of a few, very selected moments in my life. I feel small and insignificant now beside her and allow myself to feel this deeply, surrendering to both her knowledge and her grace, wondering if I truly have what it takes.

    I think of St. Teresa of Avila. Is this what it was like? Did she come to this point of personal intolerability? I am so irritated with my own mediocrity, ashamed of my inaction, disgusted with the safety I have tolerated thus far. I have more to give, and the time has come. I need to let go of what I know of myself, to move forward, to trust someone else and to give up the control. This is no longer about me and what I can do well. I need to be the medium, to spread the message this woman has given the world. She is a leader, teaching even in her death. My purpose now is to allow for this transfer, to stop the self-indulgence and to listen, to be truly present to the lesson. I have the ability to let the world know. Any former accumulation of power and prestige I have acquired in my career is not without purpose; I can use its influence now to my full potential. I can make this happen. As I arrange the grass at the foot of Karina's grave, I know that now I have a reason.

"I am you, and you are me," I declare out loud to myself, and to Karina.

If only I could have learned these lessons earlier in my life. I recall the countless trips home for the sole purpose of visiting the cemetery, only never to go in. If it resembled this place, perhaps, I would have gone. I know, however, that this current justification is only an excuse. I had no intention. My action or inaction did not matter, however. My visits were completely irrelevant. My success or failure at sitting alongside their headstone was not going to control their destiny. I had no power in bringing them back. They were gone, and my idiotic behaviour, trying in my senseless and childish way to control a situation that had already happened, would not bring them back. I reacted as a child, desperately trying to get my own way and have never been able to forgive myself for this. If only I had been there, I could have saved them. What I failed to acknowledge is, these were only the thoughts of a child. There was nothing I could have done to change their destiny, or mine. There was nothing I could have done to save them. Because of the pain I felt that day, however, the same that severed my heart directly in two and left me raw and completely helpless, I created a world where I controlled everything in my path and one in which I would never let chaos rule again. It is now time for me to release.

I leave the cemetery and decide to pick up a few groceries at the supermarket before heading home. The store is packed with people. Patiently, I wait in line, a practice I seem to have developed here. Being in a place now, however, where time does not hold the same cut-throat and demanding significance, I see people enjoying their life and really do feel less of a need for all the great rush.

Gathering my purchases, I leave the store and step back into the square. The temperature has shifted, and the wind has picked up. I watch the yellow bottoms of the palms turn, feeling a change in the weather quickly approaching. A few specks of rain foreshadow what is soon to come. Mopeds begin to rapidly race past with women clinging tightly as their patterned skirts blow behind, and I, too, quickly grab the first taxi, knowing with the increase of the pace in the street that a downpour is soon to follow.

∞∞∞∞∞∞∞∞

Late afternoon the rains hit hard. I sit in front of the thatched awning with the patio doors wide open to experience the beauty of the storm, watching the waves come crashing in and reading a book on Mayan mythology. The Mayans believed Ixchel, their goddess of fertility, represented women and childbirth, but she was also known for her tumultuous and great destructive storms, which served to cleanse the earth of its evil. Her two personae, they believed, granted the same purpose, rebirth and renewal, an opportunity to start fresh and new.

Positioned in a bamboo woven chair, with my bare feet on a cushioned footstool and sandals toppled on the floor beside me, I sit all afternoon, understanding why Karina had lived here. Perhaps she had never known the reason for coming to this island in the beginning, but she was certainly well aware of her reasons for staying.

The white-capped waves roll in to intermingle like a group of energetic six-year-old children playing twister at their first slumber party, running toward each other with their agile bodies and collapsing only at the point of exhaustion. So much of my life has been tangled and for so long, I think, as I begin to allow the ropes to slowly loosen around me. Seeing the pieces of their frayed ends that are undeniably mine, and the evil I have wished upon others, I am beginning to realize the only person I have sentenced is myself.

My father is now my only remaining family. I am embarrassed, and probably not yet completely ready to admit it, but I am beginning to see the decisions I once made as a child about the ways of the world and who my father really was may not entirely be the only truth that exists. I had never permitted the space for his reasons. I had never allowed him to explain what life was really like for him.

I sit all afternoon in a pair of shorts, barefoot in a loose linen smock at the ocean's tumultuous edge, watching the waves pound onto the shore, feeling for my father for the first time in a very long time, needing nothing more and wanting nothing less, except him here with me right now. Mist from the water blows its moistness toward me and lightly dampens my face as its breeze spreads goosebumps over my entire body and a chill clear to my spine.

As I fall asleep, Ixchel secretly reaches in without my knowing and cleans off a new space just for me and my dad.

I wake again just after 6:30 p.m. Jasmine and I are to meet Manuel and Carlos for the best lobster in town tonight at Casa di Maria at 8:00 p.m. Maria, who is a friend of one of the greatest fisherman this side of the Yucatan, is holding a special dinner tonight, and we are all lucky enough to be invited for the celebration of his successful day. Storms are often the best times for a catch, I have learned.

I prepare for the evening.

ELEVEN

Karma is the external assertion of human freedom...our thoughts, our words and deeds are the threads of the net which we throw around ourselves.

—Swami Vivekananda

After dinner, Manuel and I take a walk through the cobblestone streets, avoiding any further caffeine overload, as Jasmine and Carlos sit with their third cup of Mexican coffee with Maria and her fisherman friend, Rafael. The streets are now darkened with a light glimmer from the houses nearby. The faded red and loosely mortared cement blocks that make up the road are crooked and crumbled, but still manage to strategically capture within their trap a significant number of warm pockets from the afternoon storm. Despite their disorderly arrangement, I attempt to avoid their wetness and jump onto the flat surfaces, skipping over the puddles that lie stagnant at our feet. Manuel laughs at me and stops to remove his shoes, rolling his jeans to the knee and gently reaches to release the straps of my sandals, as well.

"Ms. Natalie, you need to feel the water. You can't avoid it," he says as he holds my shoe and loosens its clasp.

Looking back up at me, he informs me, "You're just going to get wet, senorita."

I recall the message of the fortune teller from the beach on my last trip to the Caribbean, when she spoke of a young maiden, barefoot and willing to walk alongside me. Perhaps, she was mistaken and actually meant a young Mayan, I think, as Manuel looks at me and gently removes my shoes. I take his guidance. He is right; there is no avoiding here.

A quiet genuineness lingers after the storm. After the long and violent end of its rumble, there is an innocence, a beginning, like a second chance, and an opportunity to start over. I could spend years researching this island and the dramatic effect its governing goddess once held upon its civilization, but only in being here after a storm, feeling the water embrace my feet, could I ever truly understand what it means to be touched by Ixchel's power.

"The storm provides many lessons, Ms. Natalie. There's always something to learn," Manuel schools me.

Warm water circles around my ankles like a calming bath as we walk down the street. Learning has always been a priority of mine, to have all the information, to be prepared and in control, but here, the lesson available is only found in the experience, with only one prerequisite—being here. Physical touch does not exist in a document.

I place my hand securely around Manuel's arm; he is a man who seems to be aware of the essentials of life, a man I barely know and, yet, one who seems to know me all too well. He is a good friend and wise to the ways of the world and the conditions of the heart. Walking alongside me, he guides me and ensures my strong and solid foothold in every large puddle.

∞∞∞∞∞∞∞∞

Later in the evening, when I am back at the beach house by myself, the power flickers twice and then goes out entirely. Looking out the window from here and as far as I can tell, the whole island is now black. The only glimmer of light remaining is coming from the moon overhead. Grabbing the matches in the glass jar on top of the stove, I light the candles on the table and pick up my laptop to review the work Dane emailed to me earlier this afternoon. Much like home, I am alone again and working.

Perhaps it's because I am sitting in the dark at this early-1950s pale yellow kitchen table with its aluminum legs and four plastic padded chairs, which I am sure you can only find now at a vintage shop or a really bad garage sale, but I feel peaceful in the simplicity and almost wish I could go back in time, when there was less and I knew more. The four white candles on the saucer in the middle of the table serve as my only source of light, and the sound of the ocean plays as my music in the background. I sit quietly, focusing on the four small flames and watch as their embers rise until the smoke from their individual flints become one, realizing how hidden in the chaos I have become.

I am not quite sure when it happened, but at some point I decided work is where I belonged. Portraying myself as a slave to the drudgery, work served as my ally and kept me safe, slightly on the outside and always with a very qualified and legitimate reason. Even at the moment of explaining my rationale, I could see the disappointment in the faces of my loved ones and, yet, I continued only to drive the knife deeper—like I was up to something so terribly important. I even justified my behaviour, claiming my father's work ethic as my own.

You have to work hard to get anywhere in life. If you don't work hard, you're not normal. It's expected of all good people.

I was going to be a good person, damn it. I was going to work hard and make a life of it. On very special occasions when I felt my absence absolutely inexcusable, I shifted impossible circumstances of deadlines and appointments to be present at events, to illustrate I was a powerful woman in control of my life. See Nate change the world. See Nate give up important work to be with us. What I neglected to notice, however, was this made a lot of work available in my life but did not provide me with any access to a life that worked.

My circumstances were arranged to forever shout the necessity of agenda and the pretence of importance, creating these perpetual strings that endlessly tied me into more and more involvement and continuously thwarted my actual participation in anything of any significance to me. These situations justified my absence and covered my whereabouts at all times, but what they failed to do was to reveal the truth and provide me with any real meaning.

My lesson was as recent as Manuel. I could have easily missed meeting him that morning on my way to the restaurant. If I had been in my normal state of mind, busy and on purpose, I wouldn't have spared the time for casual shopping. Feeling the intimacy of the friendship I felt tonight walking alone on the road with him, however, I am beginning to get a sense of what my life has been lacking.

I always need a buffer, a cushion to deflect and hold the distance. I never seem to take the risk and involve myself completely. I can't tolerate the idea of being busted open like a flattened steel factory after an explosion, seeing millions of burnt silver pieces of myself strewn over the plant floor and standing like a snivelling child, trusting some skilled metal worker might be able to put me all back together. We all know how well that went with Julian. I refuse to depend on someone else for my happiness, but the truth is, I don't know how and I have created this unbearable place inside of myself, with an accumulation so daunting that I refuse to face it and, in fact, use it as a comfort at some level.

I think of Julian. I blamed the complete failure of our relationship on him, on his lack of commitment and his unwillingness to be open and honest with me. The truth is, I couldn't be real with myself. I was the one afraid of the closeness and the one who was refusing to deal with the pain. I was the one who claimed I would not be affected and the only one who was declining to change. Julian never had a chance.

I lay my papers aside and walk to the window. Watching the water outside, I question why can it not be simple, why can it not just be as uncomplicated as this. The mist from the ocean drifts through the open screen and dampens my legs. I am tired of pretending. I can form a communication strategy to save an entire empire, yet cannot begin to create one simple, personal campaign for myself. Like my father, or at least the man I remember, I have become distant and aloof and unable to open up to the very people who provide me with the greatest joy. Life has become a department store for me. People, places, emotions are all organized by section with strategically shaped and solidly designed spaces for each experience and occasion. I have had every inch of life arranged within fine lines and a clear boundary, which has accounted for everything, almost. The work has to stop. I have to find my life, my real life.

I curl into the side of the sofa and bend my knees into my chest, wrapping my arms tightly around my legs and fall sleep.

∞∞∞∞∞∞∞

Saturday, I decide I will spend the day as a tourist and travel through all the local shops in the downtown core and buy a few things for the people in my life, my first step in my new personal plan of action. I will have an excuse to see them and something to say. It isn't the greatest of all plans, but it's a start. Jasmine is working all day, and we have arranged to meet everyone at the Big Palapa later tonight.

Once in the centro and browsing through the vendors' shops, I quickly discover that I have no idea what to buy. I have lost my foothold and my connection. I no longer have any idea what people's interests are or their ages might be or how many children they have, if they have any at all. I pick up a jade necklace from the glass counter in front of me and try and think what could have possibly been so dreadfully important. I think back to Julian when he said he had misplaced his first painting, and how I questioned him about how he could possibly lose the most important thing in his life. I now have a better picture, as I come to realize that I have lost most of what is important to me, Julian included.

I got lost in the purpose, setting out to make people happy and, in the end, losing this vision for them and for myself. The lessons I chose to learn over the years were of work. I picked my father's lesson instead of my own. Every choice I made was in resistance to him and, yet, here I am, still blaming him for everything I have never accomplished in life. I begin to see the absurdity as I stand now accusing a man who has no idea where I even am at this moment in life and, yet, I am holding him responsible for my inability to purchase a few appropriate trinkets for some old friends.

I decided a long time ago that I did not deserve to be with people and, in fact, the people I loved, died. It was best for all involved that I stay busy. I could handle things, not people. I could not protect them. They should not look to me for support or affection. I was not a leader of people, nor even a lover of one. It was best that I work.

It wasn't the people who were choking the life out of me, I am beginning to finally realize, but the asinine details I submerged myself in to keep myself busy and away from them. I refused to remove the buffer. I was convinced that I needed the safeguard to survive, to absorb the shock and reduce the pain and that, more importantly, so did they.

I take a deep breath and return the necklace back to the counter and straighten its heavy stone, aligning it perfectly with the corner of the counter and directly touching the adjacent jewellery, leaving no space in between. I leave the shops and enter a café two doors down and sit on the patio ledge, watching the people in the street.

"Hola, limonada por favor con agua mineral," I request as the waiter approaches me.

"Ah si, senorita," he replies and walks toward the bar.

I made a clear decision as a child. My mother died. Brendan died. I was unable to save them. Instead of forgiving myself, I created an entire life where I did not have to be alive. I became a dead woman. And now, as an adult, I have been doing whatever it takes to ensure I stay that way. It isn't other people I can't trust—it's me.

The waiter returns with my lemonade.

"Gracias, senor."

"De nada," he replies in an upward beat and lightly brushes my chin with his thumb and forefinger, holding the point of my skin just long enough for me to look deep into his eyes and even deeper into myself.

I smile back at him, grateful for his more-than-timely compassion, allowing me to take the time to forgive another small piece of myself.

I turn to enviously watch the people and the vendors, alive and animated, passing in the street, and focus on the musician sitting in a chair out front and directly facing me, wholeheartedly strumming his guitar with every piece of his heart, his voice now stirring new hope within mine.

TWELVE

One always learns one's mystery at the price of one's innocence.

—Robertson Davies

Tonight is the festival at the Big Palapa, a ritual celebration of the full moon held in the thatched dance hall at the top of the old, abandoned hotel site facing the ocean. With Hurricane Gilbert, the half-finished site is much like a transformation left unattained, like a butterfly forever caught in the life of a caterpillar, never to realize its full, promised intention. On the night of the full moon, however, it becomes the perfect playground enlightened by the gods, and a mystical, magical ballroom for all who attend.

Ixchel, well-known as the goddess of fertility and childbirth, was also revered as the moon goddess by the Mayans and returns on a monthly cycle, spreading her light and granting her people vision, leaving them both inspired and new.

We all meet out front, under the old, beaten sign that hangs on a slant and reads, "The Big Palapa."

A nine piece mariachi band plays centre stage as we walk up the old staircase and enter the open balcony. The room is scattered with several dark wooden wagon wheels with their rust-coloured centres and glass circle tops. The bar at the northwest corner is a smooth, moon-shaped surface lined with a number of backless, orange leather stools. Their seats are thick and their legs thin, like a chicken-legged worker with a beer pot belly, not necessarily appealing to the eye, but old, familiar and surprisingly very comfortable.

The floor is made of large rounded rocks that have been flattened and mortared between to provide a smooth surface. Several old sets of tables and chairs are dotted throughout, leaving space for a sizeable dance floor in the middle of the room, encircling the band. Sitting low over each table are handmade pottery lamps, each with cheap tea light candles in their centre that seem to be going out simultaneously, keeping the servers busy. Hundreds of tiny, white lights are also woven among the bamboo thatch, providing a warm glow with sufficient light until the moon is in full force. And the moon hovers now behind the darkened clouds like a special guest awaiting introduction.

In exchange for a few pesos, the lady at the front door smiles as she hands each of us a clay pottery cup, our bottomless container for all the free tequila-laden lime juice we can handle. I take a sip of the heavily injected punch, knowing its lethal free-flow will need to be respected.

"Up for a lesson?" I tease Manuel once we secure a table and the next band begins.

"Ah ha! Senorita, LA SALSA!" he demands, full of life and clapping his hands above his head, with a grin the size of large moon crater.

I own my body dancing with him now, moving and feeling myself from the inside, feeling the richness, the fullness in nothing. The luxury of each moment is tangible and, yet, something that cannot be found in the surroundings. Getting to the source of what has been stopping me in the past and identifying what I now might desire, I have space, space to hear my long-awaited true self speak. My dancing has become an expression of my sensuality. I am free and aware of being alive, and the strangest thing is, the actual physical movement is only such a small part of this bursting energy that is originating from within. Manuel still continues to teach me with each step as he unleashes the rhythm of his soul.

After hours of dancing in the mystical moonlight at the Big Palapa, we finally call it a night, just before 3:00 a.m., and Jasmine and I make our way back to her house. She has invited me to stay with her tonight, since my place is too long a walk in the dark, and the taxis will all be occupied with the huge influx of people in the centro from the party.

The two of us pioneer our way through the darkness, along the path back to her house. We have spent the past few weeks creating a real bond together, well beyond business or that of any client and editor. We have become close friends, spending most of our days and evenings together. I respect her. She has brought a lot of valuable introductions into my life, causing me to break new personal ground, learning lessons not only about the world and people, but also about what it truly means to be alive and happy, and myself. I guess this is what people mean when they say we meet soul mates in life, people who help to further us along on our path. The time is nearing when I will soon need to return home. I am going to miss her and our daily get-togethers.

∞∞∞∞∞∞∞∞

Once at the house, we enter to find the electricity has gone out again. We decide to take a few minutes to unwind down by the ocean before turning in for the night. Jasmine grabs us each a bottle of water from the fridge, and we head out the back door, through the garden and down the small palm-covered pathway to the beach.

"Check out that moon," I comment as I sit down and dig my feet into the damp, sugary-white sand, staring out at its big, bright light reflecting on the water.

Jasmine hums in mutual delight.

"Do you see the rabbit?" she asks.

"I've never seen that before," I respond, surprised.

"The rabbit in the moon," she says by way of introducing her story.

Jasmine explains to me how the Aztecs believed that their god, Quetzalcoatl, once came to earth as a man and set out on a long journey. After many days of traveling without food, Quetzalcoatl thought he would die, until the rabbit came along and offered himself as food. In expression of his gratefulness, he said he would always ensure that the world remembered the rabbit and placed the animal's image in the moon, so that all men could see the rabbit for all time.

In the Mayan story of creation, the *Popol Vuh*, the Hero twins outsmarted the Lords of Death and ascended to heaven, where one became the Sun and the other became the Moon. In order to darken the light of the other brother, the one twin threw a rabbit to dim the other's light, and now the Moon is always the less bright of the two.

"It's amazing how clearly you can see it," I say, shocked at its distinct outline. "I would never have seen it until you pointed it out."

"Sometimes it takes someone else to see something you can never see for yourself," she teases.

"Sometimes it does." I smile.

And I can. I can see the rabbit, with its long floppy ears and its full-cheeked face, sitting with its round belly and its big bushy tail. We sit in silence, breathing in the night's nourishment.

After several minutes, Jasmine turns to me and asks, "What's somethin' you always wanted to know, but never knew—like a secret you were never able to find out?"

"I don't know." I laugh lightly. "That's a pretty big question."

"Anything," she offers.

"What about you?" I deflect her question without even noticing.

"Always wanted to know why Fin cheated."

"Who's Fin?"

"You're avoiding my question."

"OK, truly?" I pause to reflect, before taking a long breath and think deeply.

"The relationship between my Auntie Kaila and my mother," I say, surprised at my own response.

"You think they had something?" Jasmine questions, suggesting a concept I am not sure I am willing to address.

"Maybe," I honestly admit for the first time.

"Does it matter if they did?" she asks.

"I don't know," I answer, feeling awkward and in wonder.

I squint my eyes tight, pinching the bridge of my nose with my thumb and middle finger, and try to concentrate. Staring out at the ocean, I immerse myself in my own inquiry, while Jasmine silently sits and looks at me. Her unwavering intensity and unending patience provide a space for me to be honest and allow me to bring another layer of myself to the surface. I know she can hear me at a level at which I cannot even hear myself, and I am willing to open up to her wisdom.

"I'm not sure, Jas," I say slowly, realizing for the first time I don't know what the issue is or why it is of any real importance to me at all, but I do know that I want to somehow understand what constantly has me starting and stalling and wondering and frozen.

"I don't think it's so much about the relationship and what might have been, but more about the secrets and the things she didn't share with you."

I take a deep, heavy breath and feel myself sink deeper into the sand beneath me. She is right. It is the secrets. There were many things I didn't understand. And it is not only her secrets now, but also mine. My biggest fear is that my mind would rather die with these obscurities inside than admit the truth and allow my heart to truly feel.

I think again of Sofia, the fortune teller on the beach, and what she had said to me at my reading years ago.

Not that she was weak, your mother . . . she just couldn't find a means of communicatin' her feelings, couldn't deal with the pressure . . . You're much like her, but you're strong, indestructible. You've got a power, great power.

"I'm afraid of the anger," I confess to Jasmine.

"You're afraid of your power," she challenges. "You're just using the anger to cover it up."

Jasmine, too, had been there before and she knew. She is right. The anger is my way out and keeps me busy and consumed, distracted from moving beyond to anything else. For years, this anger has been raging and swirling inside, so loudly that, at times, I feel as if I am nothing else. I have managed to a certain extent, but know I'm on a fast track to a slow death without any real commitment to do anything about it, feeling as if my time has already come and gone. Attempting to run from myself, yet all the while standing still and twisted, I have become wound so acutely inside that I am rotting from the inside out, rancid with blood and blame and betrayal.

All I have to do is admit the anger, and the rest will take care of itself, but I won't, and there is a constant lurking darkness knocking, warning me. Every time it rises to be acknowledged, I bury it further down, and thus the negativity vibrates at lower and lower levels. Soon, my silent fury will be all that exists, forcing me into more seclusion to conceal its ugliness. The secret is, I hate myself for feeling this and have been poisoning my mind and my body with constant denial, which only serves to drive me further into the dark abyss.

"What do you think will happen, if you just let go?" Jasmine inquires.

"I have no idea," I respond sadly and honestly, tired of carrying the excuses and exhausted with all the lies.

"What will happen if you just tell yourself the truth?"

"I don't know the truth."

"You know the truth."

"I don't know the truth," I insist.

"You know the truth," Jasmine says quietly again as she takes the heel of her hand and reaches to rub the full length of my back from the base upward, quietly encouraging the venom to exit.

I do know the truth. I begin to live the longest and, perhaps, most loathsome moments of my life, realizing now how much of it has been paralyzed by my own fear of feeling. Time ceases. The conversation in my head ceases. There is nothing but silence. All I feel now is Jasmine's hand as she continues to motion this ugliness forward, beckoning, calling, commanding. I prepare to deal with a part of me that I have never been courageous enough to address on my own. I accept her compassion, although still fighting at some level to contain my emotion. My heart beats loudly now, with the fear begging itself free and this primal indicator telling me it is time to surface. I hold my breath, thinking I should feel stupid, and yet I don't. All I feel is her friendship and her unwillingness to give up until I am capable of full release. I stop resisting and exhale, breathing out through my mouth and begin to let this large funnel of torment unravel.

"You're not alone, Natalie. You're never alone."

I have spent so much of my life protected and on purpose and hiding from this very fact. I have built an entire life with the facade of independence and busyness, to conceal any and all real emotion. Eventually I allow the secrets to surface and begin to feel the pain I have inflicted upon myself. No one else is torturing me, no one else ever has.

In this moment, I allow Jasmine to be my mother and Brendan. She is family and loss. She is fear and intimacy. She is stillness and honesty. She has taken me back to the edge of those two mahogany boxes in the church years ago, to the time I was unwilling to face and when I refused to tell the truth.

Finally, I force out my painful confessions to Jasmine, and the truth is, I blamed my mother and Brendan for dying— it was their fault. If they hadn't died, I would still be able to love, I would have a life. I hated them for dying and I hated myself even more for feeling this way. I did not deserve to be happy and I designed a life where I could continually destroy any chance of it. In reality, I am the one who stopped feeling that day. I am the one who harvested the rage. The truth is, I loved deeply, with every ounce of my heart, and I lost. Instead of leaving myself open to feel this pain, I am the one who walked away and betrayed myself.

I inhale deeply and surrender to all the emotion I have been trying to kill off within my own heart, soon to discover that when I allow this and I allow Jasmine to help me, I can reach places far beyond anything I can ever get to on my own.

"Are you willing to let people love you, Natalie?" Jasmine asks. "You have a world of people who want to, but are you willing?"

I remain silent and contemplate my entire future in this world and in this moment. I sit from an outsider's point of view, still vacant and unattached, but even as stone-faced as I appear, I feel the passion seeping into my bloodstream and begin to feel a drum tap from deep inside my heart.

"Do you know what the key to understanding the Mayan prophecies is?" Jasmine calmly asks, both tolerant and accepting of my non-reactive behaviour and, I suspect, knowing on some level that I am about to burst like a bud in the hot spring sun.

"No," I quietly admit.

"The real key is recognizing that human thinking is not something that takes place inside your head, in isolation. It's understanding we're all one. When you hurt, I hurt. Your pain is my pain. You're not alone, you are never alone."

"In Lak 'ech."

"Yes, In Lak 'ech. I am you, and you are me," Jasmine agrees.

My heart beats slower now, but still loudly, taking solid and sure steps toward its creeping expansion. The fear gradually dissipates. I let it go. I finally let it all go and begin to allow a space of compassion for myself, feeling my heart open, feeling relief. Jasmine is right—life can change in a moment. This is my moment; it is time for me to choose life.

I am the only one who ever prevented this release from happening any earlier, thinking I was different, special somehow, that my experience was unlike any other. My error in this, I have learned, is not that we are not all special, but that we are all uniquely special. Life is not a competition—it's a gift. We are all one, but we are all each unique. Until we can understand this and accept this for ourselves, we are stuck trying to prove our specialness over another or hiding from the fact that we think we do not quite make the mark.

Because of what happened years ago, I thought I was different. Other people's mothers and brothers didn't die on them; mine did. I was different, I wasn't like other people. I wasn't meant to be loved.

"Are you willing to let go and let people love you?" Jasmine asks again, knowing I need to take this step and declare it for myself.

I feel my mind still trying to fight to hold on. No matter what I want, or how much, my stubbornness is still trying to keep me separate and alone. I have finally decided, however, that it is time to end this struggle and accept something bigger.

"Yes," I finally commit to Jasmine who, I know, will hold me to this and not allow me to falter in my promise.

Jasmine turns and hugs me, and I feel her face smile on my cheek. I thank my mother and Brendan for being part of my life and promise now to live life, loving, and to declare another chapter in my life complete. I take a deep breath as I think of Sofia once again and what she had said to me on the beach.

Sometimes you gotta put all your cards on the table.

I close my eyes, quietly knowing I have just played my entire hand for all now to see. No more games, no more lying; my life has finally become real. I am now accountable to Jasmine for keeping my promise and also responsible for making Karina's dream come alive; I owe this to all of us. It is no longer just me; we are now a team.

Jasmine explains that to have all your desires become alive and real, you must first clean your heart and be honest with yourself. She found a way to cleanse the emotional poison from her life and her mind. She found the things that made her happy and her true source of joy and spent her life consciously putting these into practice every day. She found a way to get back to herself. It was time for me to create the life I loved, rather than the one I was constantly trying to avoid.

I understand now why my mother had insisted on her visits with Auntie Kaila. There is an understanding available between women, not found in any other realm. And sometimes, the secrets we bury are so ugly and unreachable, we feel as if we are trapped, forced to live their vicious shame and constant defeat. What I have learned, however, is that the unconditional love of a true soul sister can shine a light on your path and have you see things you've never been able to see before, and finally set you free. Like the rabbit in the moon, it has always been there, but without Jasmine, I never would have seen the truth.

After a few more minutes, we finally decide to head back into the house. Jasmine shows me to my room, and I get ready now for bed. The night is hot and humid. Unable to fall asleep right away, I lie awake recalling our entire conversation from earlier and eventually get up and go to the bathroom. Focusing as much as I can, I make my way through the dark, feeling the contours of the furniture and quietly moving into the hall, dragging my hand along the wall and over a large wooden frame hanging just outside of the bathroom. I bend closer to the surface to gain a better view of the picture but am unable to make out its image. I enter the bathroom and shut the door quietly behind me.

∞∞∞∞∞∞∞∞

In the morning, I wake just before eight to the smell of fresh coffee. The electricity has obviously been restored in the night, as Jasmine is now up and busy making breakfast. I head to the kitchen to join her.

"Buenos dias," she says cheerfully. "Nice pitcher of cold water in the fridge."

"Buenos dias, gracias," I respond, pouring myself a tall glass.

Jasmine sits at the table with her coffee. I stand at the kitchen counter and swallow quietly. The water hits the back of my throat like a tidal wave to a sandy beach. I feel its path reach the dehydrated stretch of my body and sink in almost instantaneously.

"Just what I needed." I exhale in relief.

"Hungry?" Jasmine asks.

"Absolutely."

"Coffee?" she offers, handing me a piping mugful.

"Thank you." I turn and accept the cup and set my glass on the counter.

Jasmine divides a more than generous helping of huevos rancheros that she has been cooking on the stove and separates the eggs onto two plates for us.

"Who is Fin?" I inquire, taking another sip of my coffee and hoping to continue our conversation from last night.

"Guy my girlfriend dated, promoter, real playboy. Constantly looking for the next deal. Girls were like his beer, the more the merrier, whether for socializing or for other purposes. Strangely enough, when either got too heavy, he stopped indulging or simply changed brands."

I laugh at her analogy, knowing the type quite well and smiling at her uncanny ability to state the bare and the blatant.

"Couldn't understand why he would ever cheat on her. They were perfect."

"So, what happened?"

"She got tired of the lies, I guess."

"It's a race. Then you wonder, for what," I agree, having experienced the chase a couple of times myself.

"Empty," she states blankly.

"Empty, yes." I blink in agreement, feeling almost aloof, and wonder if I understand her meaning and whether she has ever experienced the kind of relationships that I have had, ones defined by ambition, money, prestige, or even work schedules. I am well-aware of the vacancy, the nothingness and the gaping hole that later screams inside of you.

"And then you give it up, only wanting a better life for yourself, and you're left with a crater of guilt that you have just robbed your mother of her only chance to have a decent life," Jasmine continues as I nod my head, knowing all too well the struggle to have it all and the whining voices telling me I was too hard to please.

"Karina thought the best way to measure your compatibility was to do a puzzle together."

"A puzzle?"

"Her theory was that, on the first date, you should do a puzzle together. If you couldn't sit and build something as simple as that, then there was no chance of building any type of future. If you fought over the pieces, it meant he'd never develop his own interests outside of you and would eventually drive you mad. If he kept asking your opinion of which piece was next, he was irresponsible and would never initiate action of his own. If, however, the two of you could communicate, work independently, yet still toward a common goal, you had a chance."

"Now, there's a theory."

"Makes a lot of sense, no?"

"Yes, it certainly does," I agree calmly.

"Let me show you around," Jasmine says as she places our empty plates in the sink and directs me into the next room.

"This is my living room," she says proudly. "Always wanted one with a swing. People call them living rooms and then arrange them so you can barely breathe in 'em. I wanted to play in mine," she reveals.

Undeniably, she has done just that, and there in the corner of the room is a mini-hammock swing hanging from the ceiling, with its white-and-red netted seat. I shake my head and smile at her. She is definitely one of a kind.

"Climb on," Jasmine encourages.

"I want one of these," I respond.

"You can have whatever you want." She smirks.

"Last night—" I start.

"Si, no?" Jasmine responds, understanding me without any explanation.

I swing and watch her reflection in the mirror on the wall in front of us.

"It was the first time, I—"

"Felt," she says. "*Felt* is the word."

"Forgave them," I confess.

"And yourself. You allowed space for yourself, Natalie."

"Yeah, I did," I admit.

"You surrendered. And once you can do that, that's where your life is."

I take her wisdom, not as one more thing I need to know, but as a gift, thinking if we could only refer to people as presents and look for the special lessons they have to teach us, rather than constantly analyzing whether what they are saying is right or wrong, we could create such an abundance of love and light in our lives. And it is true: I did surrender last night. I let it all out and allowed someone into my little corner of the world, without knowing any outcome. I let nothing stand between Jasmine and me for those few thick moments—no wall, no shield, no boundary. I removed my buffer and let her in.

"Every house needs one of these," I say as I extend my legs and tighten my arms back to thrust myself into the air, trying to remember the last time I was in a playground.

"Playing's where it's at, *chica*. Come on, I'll give you the grand tour!" she says as she swings her arm inviting me.

We make our way through the rest of the house as she describes the various origins of her eclectic pieces of contemporary Mexican folk art. We enter the hall, where she explains that the framed picture hanging on her wall near the bathroom is one of the paintings Karina left her when she died: "Her son painted it when he was a boy. She loved it. Of everything she left, this was the one thing that meant more to her than anything else."

Jasmine's words begin to fall distant in a faint echo, like tiny pebbles being thrown over a high mountain top, flying away and into thin air, until I can barely hear her voice at all. As we approach the painting, I hear nothing but a stilled silence, like an abandoned gymnasium after school has been dismissed for vacation, hollow and empty. I can only stand and stare, and hear minute whispers of her story now in the background. I cannot move or breathe. All I can do is let my body drop against the wall behind me for support. I stand and look at the frame in front of me until it is only a fuzzy image with a thick, dark border.

"Yeah, she said her son painted it. Said he was only five or six at the time."

With my own voice barely able to surface, I absently whisper, "Six."

"Did I tell you that story?" she responds with slight confusion.

"No."

"No? Well, how do you know?" she questions me.

"Julian."

"What?" she says, dragging out her response.

"The child . . . was Julian."

What hangs before me is a painting of long swathes of green lushness, simple and magnificent. The painting is bright, fun, adventurous and free—everything he described to me on the morning after the first night we ever spent together. The mysterious painting I fumbled over last night in the dark was the willow tree, and it was brilliant. I had found the missing piece of Julian's life.

Just as Karina suggested completing a puzzle to ensure compatibility, Jasmine and I sit to put together a story that has been long in search of completion. In my greatest attempt to escape him, his incredible story has found his way to me. Like Julian, as much as I tried to deny the feelings of the past, they have been magically weaving their way to find me all along. In the end, and without even conscious effort, I have been provided with all that I ever truly wanted—the real story.

THIRTEEN

Start by doing what's necessary, then what's possible, and suddenly you are doing the impossible.

—Saint Francis

The sky is blue with a black outline. I see the structure. The blue is brilliant and warm. The black is the mountains, the rocks and the trees. The blue is open and inviting. I grab the black and pull myself forward. I place my foot upon the black and rise. The black has supported me to get here, but now fades and is no more. I have reached the surface. The blue welcomes me. I am not afraid. I take my first step into the deep blue.

∞∞∞∞∞∞∞∞∞

I awake smiling, ecstatic that my dream has ended in blue. I take my coffee and go outside to sit by the ocean as the sun comes up and hear a rooster now crowing in the distance. Watching the waves gently rolling in on the beach, I see a small group of birds on the rocks and observe their instinctual interactions. I have heard that when the babies are young, a mother bird has been known to abandon the nest. As I watch the babes screech tiny cries from their small, fleece-lined necks and the mother, with her skilled beak, place her mouth delicately inside theirs to give them food, I wonder how. She is their lifeline. How could a bird that nurses her young so carefully leave them unattended with little hope for survival?

There are demons that lurk among the heavy sighing trees of the forest and wait in the darkness. A mother bird can sense these dangers and often be faced with the choice to stay and be killed or flee into the night. Knowing her babies are too young to fly, it is the hardest decision she has to make as she tucks them tightly into their small, straw home, until she can return again. But often, when the darkness fades and she circles back, she finds her babies have been claimed by the humans who live nearby. She suffers, knowing that humans will never truly be able to teach her young the ways of the bird. These young babes will now always be in search of something they will not even know they lack, the true heart of the bird. I breathe deeply and smell the newness of the morning.

Whether there is a future for Julian and I or not, and no matter what has transpired between the two of us, I need to let him know. I go back inside, place my mug on the counter and stare at the telephone. Afraid and nervous, I finally dial, wondering what his response will be, excited to tell him the truth, and praying another woman does not answer the phone.

"Julian?"

"Nate?" We both stall in silence before he continues.

"Everything OK?"

I have not heard his voice in months, not since the night he left me sitting in the wine room at Da Vinci's. My anger automatically resurfaces.

OK? Is everything OK? No, you bastard, everything is not OK. You dumped me, if you don't remember, with no valid excuse or apparent concern for how I might deal with the pain. You ripped my entire world away from me and left me with nothing but a three-month depression and a drinking problem. No, everything is not OK.

I stop all the surfacing feelings that are immediately rising and sit silent, carefully gathering my thoughts before I say anything further. That was then; this is now. I need to leave the anger in the past, where it belongs, and I have to let him know why I am calling.

"You need to come here," I finally reply.

"Where? Are you all right?" he responds with the empathy I have known from him before.

"Yes, I'm fine," I calmly and honestly admit, now forgiving him and ready to hand him the key to his past. "Julian, I found the willow."

"You what?"

I explain where I am and after a couple of phone calls back and forth with him, we have arranged for him to arrive within two days. Within forty-eight hours he will have his answers, his own final completion to years of unanswered questions. In just listening to the tone of his voice, I can hear his relief. He will now have the opportunity to end decades of heartache and wondering, to finally hear the truth for himself.

After our call, I sit back down at the kitchen table, thinking of family and forgiveness and about all the things we need to do for each other, and know there is another call I have to make. I pick up the receiver and dial.

"Hello," the voice on the other end answers.

"Dad? It's Natalie."

At first, not a great deal is said, not much ever really was, with the exception of talk about business and the weather. I explain I am on assignment in the Caribbean and the weather is hot, and I lit a candle for Mom and Brendan. He is well and busy with work and said he did the same. Although it is the same conversation we always have, a rock is turning for the two of us and that rock, I have humbly come to discover, is not my father, but me. Old issues are being left behind, and I am finally stepping out of the way. I explain what happened with Julian and the painting, and that he has finally found his mother. As I pause for a moment, my father speaks, and for the first time in a very long time, I listen to him and hear a man I have never heard before.

"Nate, I wanted to give you the world. For you to have it all."

"Dad . . ." I try to stop him, not sure that I can emotionally handle a real conversation with him right now.

"I wanted so much more for you, Nattie. I knew it would be difficult, but I wanted to give you every advantage. That's why I sent you. Your mom struggled, Nattie."

"I couldn't see that then, though," I explain, trying to help him understand the reason for my rebellion, rather than making him wrong.

"I know. You had no idea. I wasn't very good at explaining things to you, and your mom was too sad and embarrassed that she couldn't do more. You were special, though. You're the one; you were always the one. I knew from the first moment I held you."

"What do you mean?" I ask, not understanding what he is talking about.

"You have something, Nattie. You inspire people. You help them feel."

I can barely believe what my father is saying to me, especially when I know I have spent more than half of my adult life trying to kill this exact quality within myself.

"I saw the self-doubt, the anger, before your mother and Brendan died, and most certainly after. I knew you hated me for sending you to school. I just didn't know what to say or how to go about it. I was afraid to lose you."

"Well, I haven't left a hell of a lotta opportunity for you to open up, have I?"

"It doesn't matter, Nattie. None of it matters now."

"No," I swallow hard, trying to keep my emotions level. "Maybe we can get together when I get back in town? Go for dinner or something?" I suggest.

"I'd really like that."

"OK, I'll call you when I get back."

"Sounds good."

"Well, I guess I'll talk to you later then, Dad."

"Yeah."

"Dad?" I stall, not ready to hang up yet and let go of our new connection. There is a pause on the line as we both wait on each end. My stomach tenses.

"Love you, Butterfly."

"I love you too, Daddy."

In an attempt to be strong and unaffected, I place the receiver in its cradle, slowly, with as much control as my clenching hand can possibly muster, but find my bottom lip quivering uncontrollably and my knees giving out as I crumble to the floor.

Now just a small, frightened girl, I release every tear that has ever been held down. Each surfaces slowly, with excruciating pain, sharply splintering the formerly pristine fortress around my heart into a million pieces. Lying in a collapsed heap for the duration of the afternoon, I am painfully reminded of the honoured place this man holds in my life and how his small endearment melts my heart, reminding me of how special I am in his. As many barriers as I placed between us, and as much as I withheld all interaction from him, I spent my entire life waiting to hear those three words. Like a young child who sits on the edge of a curb and waits for the ice cream truck's arrival, I had never left that corner. I had been waiting my entire life for the orange-coloured Popsicle with the ice cream centre.

I am a corporate executive who works very hard to gain her position. And of all that I attempt to make of my life, Daddy's little girl is the only title I have ever truly wanted. No job, no amount of money, could ever grant me this desire. Of all that I could aspire to do or be, this is the single, solitary accomplishment that I have sought. I would never be able to admit this to him, but the simple fact is, he already knows. As much as I thought I had been healing myself over the past several years by ignoring this longing, I realize now I have merely been letting an open wound scab over. My father's words have now ripped that scar off in one swift moment, leaving me raw to bleed late into the evening, freeing me to experience pain, and to finally heal.

What I have come to understand is that the anger I once held for him so strongly did not always exist and, on its flip side it, actually contained a deep love and admiration. My anger only began the day my father sent me away, because I could not deal with my own feelings of rejection. I could not see any bigger picture at that time. All I could feel was the devastating ache of not being wanted and the terrible hole in my heart that would form from not seeing the man I loved most in the world every day.

In one simple phone call, my father reconnected me to our precious days of happiness together and to my entire life. I had spent years convincing myself I was trapped, crawling in the caterpillar's body, believing I was earthbound and broken, only to be reminded this afternoon by the never-ending faith of my father that we can all transform in a moment, and I already and always did have everything I ever needed to fly. This is not because I am a schooled and seasoned business woman, now at the ripe age of forty, but because I am, and always have been, my daddy's one and only Butterfly.

∞∞∞∞∞∞∞∞

The phone rings loudly, a rotary phone, with its noise like that from a racing ambulance through rush hour traffic, unnecessarily and inexcusably loud, but all the while essential and completely unavoidable. I fumble for the receiver. Checking my watch, I stretch the long, black phone cord across the bed, realizing I have been asleep for over two hours. I wipe the dried corners of my dehydrated mouth and lick my lips as I answer.

"Hola," I say, expecting Jasmine.

"Hey, girl."

Dane. I swear, the man has a Natalie Lauren mood metre surgically implanted. Just at the point when I feel I am furthest from reality, I can always count on him for a sense of grounding. It is not that he is even aware of my past few days; he is calling just to share his own excitement, which is exactly what I need. Relieved, I listen now as he begins to explain his recent research and how, since my departure, he has been exploring the Yucatan and its history.

"The structures, Nate."

"Incredible, aren't they?"

"Did you know the Mayans were one of the most advanced civilizations, organizing time and calendars and structures?"

"You're obsessed, aren't you?"

"Smitten. I want to make the trek. I've decided I'm going to be an explorer when I grow up."

"You always have been, hon."

"Really, I want to see these incredible ancient civilizations, to experience their brilliance and insight into humanity. I want to travel to Chichen Itza, Tulum, Coba, all through Quintana Roo and on to Belize. What do you think?"

"I don't know. How do you really feel?" I tease, smiling and happy to hear him so excited.

"I know it'll put a lot on your plate, but I'll come to the island first, touch base with you, meet Jasmine."

"Perfect."

"It won't be more than a couple of months."

I listen to his enthusiasm. I have missed him so much.

"It won't be a problem?" he asks.

"I'll see you soon. Julian's on his way down too."

"What do you mean? What's going on?"

"More than you can even imagine. I'll fill you in when you get here."

In the past twenty-four hours I have talked to the three most important men in my life, and two are en route to see me within the next two days. Maybe this place is named the Island of Women for its ability to attract men across continents, I think, or maybe because the women who come here become reconnected to their own draw. I sit, nervous and excited, confused and content.

∞∞∞∞∞∞

The guys will not be arriving for another day. Jasmine and I decide to make a trek of our own today to the cenote, and this one was definitely an islander secret. Just before noon, at the dock in front of the gas station, we meet up with the boat we have rented for the day. I am not much for small crafts heading out over rough, open ocean, but Jasmine has assured me I will not be disappointed with the trip.

Finally arriving at a crystal cave of wooden thatched huts with huge magenta trees, we are instructed to jump from the boat into the water and to make our way to the white, sandy beach. I still expect to see tourists, but there are none. There is nothing, no electricity here, no tourists, no dock, just open-air huts and a handful of inhabitants. We promise a few pesos to some very young, entrepreneurial, barefooted spirits, who lead us on our way as we hike through the tangled, narrow, dirt-trodden path, passing speckled roosters and large iguanas and the only public means of transportation on the island, which seem to be a few donkeys with a couple of old men leading their way.

Halfway there, partly due to our rugged sea ride over here, I am sure, Jasmine and I are both in need of a bathroom and then, possibly, a beverage. The youngsters lead us to the local watering hole, where we are invited into the home of the only restaurateurs on the island. When asking to use their washroom facilities, I am shockingly introduced to the most primitive accommodation I have yet to experience. The woman motions us to follow her as she leads us through the dark and into the back of her kitchen, through a hall of dirt floor, to a darkened space draped with a burlap curtain. Inside the room are the facilities, which consist of a hole in the ground. As I enter, she hands me a bowl of water and motions my instruction. I am to throw the water down the hole when I am finished. I enter the darkened space, squat and smile. No one would believe me if I told them. Later, I pass the bowl on to Jasmine as I stand at the sink to wash my hands, smirking and proud of both of us.

Once we return back outside to her small patio area, the woman of the house offers us fresh chips and salsa, and serves us the best limonada in the history of Mexico. Of all the places I have travelled, I have never experienced such genuine hospitality. Literally offering us everything they have, the couple then sits with us, as if we are their lifelong neighbours who have just come by for an afternoon visit.

Later, we leave and make our way to the site. Once reaching our destination, we find a handful of adventurous souls with whom to share the experience. Not many make it here, which is fortunate and unfortunate. We stand now, in awe. The water flow is natural and comes up from the bottom of the large pool of water, creating a small mountain of bubbles in the centre.

"Ojo de agua," Jasmine explains. "The water here is fresh water. The bubbles in the middle, they call them the eyes; they are continually pumping the water up from its source below."

"How can fresh water possibly come from salt water?" I question.

"Ah, magic," Jasmine jokes.

It is true; however, it is a mangrove in the middle of this small island where this freshwater pool exists amidst an entire ocean of salt water, just like a natural diamond in the rough. Apparently, and as explained to us by the locals, the entire Yucatan holds this type of underground water system, where the water is held in its landlocked aquifer, and separates and layers the water according to its density, allowing the whole system to be contained, serving its individual existence and purpose, yet still being completely connected to the ocean as a whole.

A young Mayan man is working on his art at the left of the water hole. His craftsmanship is immaculate. I have seen replicas back on the island, but nothing like what is before me. The embroidery is brilliant. Both Jasmine and I have no money. What little we did bring, we left for the kind woman at the last stop in appreciation of her fine hospitality. I apologize for having nothing to offer him. He informs me that he wants nothing from me and reaches beneath the table to a bag at his feet and pulls out a handcrafted flute made of wood.

"Senorita, you have come with nothing, and this is good. I have something for you," he announces.

I watch as he begins to play. His eyes are dark and seductive, his skin innocent and beautiful. I stand and accept as he plays his meticulously crafted instrument for me. His eyes are determined and intentional, and do not leave mine. He plays and all else around us falls silent to his music. I find myself feeling warmed in a way I have never felt before, as if my heart is physically heating, expanding. The music allows me to breathe deep inside of myself as I begin to understand Karina's experience of being consumed.

When he finishes, I feel honoured and renewed. I thank him. The tips of his fingers touch the skin on the top of my hand in the smallest stroke, but churn the energy inside of me like a washing machine on full tilt, wrapping around inside my entire perimeter until I am warm and full. I leave feeling whole and cleansed.

In one moment, a man whom I have never met before inspires a passion for life I will not soon forget.

"Beautiful," Jasmine says as we leave.

"Better than any performance I've ever heard in my entire life," I agree.

"People are drawn to you, Natalie."

"God, wasn't that amazing?" I say, still stunned.

Our young friends lead us back to the boat. I take one last look at the young Mayan man before leaving and find him still watching me. His hair is ebony, long and tied back, and his eyes are the same colour. His face shines; his skin is smooth, unblemished and healthy. I feel the oddest sensation of feeling both empty and full. I slowly lift my hand and wave goodbye to him as I walk quietly back along our path, feeling enlightened by his power and my own.

∞∞∞∞∞∞∞

Once we are safely back at the Jasmine's house, I pull out the plastic-wrapped prayer cards the old lady at the church gave me and ask Jasmine if she will translate them for me.

"Are you ready for what they have to say?" she asks.

"What do you mean? Have you read them before?"

"No."

"Then, what do you mean?"

"I'll read them under one condition."

"All right."

"You mind what they say."

"OK," I agree with enthusiasm and a sense of adventure.

"You should be careful what you promise, Ms. Natalie," she warns and smiles.

I knew from the way she spoke about the cards she had an understanding far deeper than I knew anything about, but I am a woman of my word and when I make a promise, I keep it.

Jasmine pulls the two cards in front of her and begins. The first is a prayer to the Virgin Mary of Guadalupe, asking for forgiveness of sins, blessings for work, and for help in the area of illness, the holy Virgin grants wishes for anything she believes to be proper. A small prayer of blessing and forgiveness—I could deal with that. The second is the prayer of the Magnificent, which glorifies God for setting his sights on his humble servants. It explains the reasons why we can be blissful and why God is omnipotent, for he has extended his mercifulness from generation to generation, using his power to pale the pride of the arrogant, interfering with their plans and stripping the powerful by raising the humble. He fills the coffers of the needy and leaves the rich without a penny. Exalting Israel, his servant, he promises his great mercy and kindness, just as he promised our fathers and all their descendants, forever and ever. Amen.

I seek to interpret its true meaning or at least to understand how it could possibly apply to me. My plans have certainly been interrupted and my pride paled. I came here arrogant and have definitely been humbled. I begin to understand the old churchwoman's message and accept my new responsibility. I am the servant to carry the message forward. People need to know Karina's story, and I am the one to deliver it.

My world feels much larger than it ever has before. Jasmine is right. This is no small task. I, however, have given my word.

FOURTEEN

Freedom is but one large step into one's own reality.

—Penny D. Burnham

The sky is blue and magical. I now not only walk, but have also learned to run. There is no more black, only blue—mystical, brilliant and full of discovery. The black is no more, yet if I stand for a moment and squint, if I make my eye very small, the world once again shows a black outline, holding a small blue sparkle in its centre, a focus point in the shape of a diamond. The diamond I have now discovered. My mission is to unveil the secret path, so that the blue may broaden and the black may fade, and that all may have the choice to step forward. Of this, I am to tell the world.

∞∞∞∞∞∞∞∞∞

I awake. Today is a new day. There is no way to regain what has been lost. There is only now, starting from here and moving forward. I could never have predicted this moment, but Julian is almost here. I pack up the last few things in my bags before heading to Jasmine's for breakfast. We will all stay as her guests tonight to relax with each other and have dinner and finally bring all of the individual pieces of our fragmented stories together.

∞∞∞∞∞∞∞∞

"Buenos dias, mi mayita."

"What does that mean?" I ask, laughing at Jasmine as she greets me at her front door.

"My little Mayan."

I smile calmly and give her a hug as I enter. She kisses my cheeks on each side and takes my bags and places them in the foyer; then we head to the kitchen.

"OK, I've been here a few of weeks and now I'm part Mayan?" I question as she hands me a cup of coffee and we sit down together at her kitchen table.

"The Maya are the carriers of the truth. They believe the first and greatest act in life is your willingness to undertake a process of personal growth—to be willing to take down the barriers between who you have become and who you really are," Jasmine informs me and pauses before continuing.

"You have done that here, Natalie. You've completed that for yourself and now you've opened the space for Julian to gain this closure as well."

"I never would have had any of this without you," I acknowledge.

"You would've found your way. Eventually, we always do. The timing just depends on how quick we are to get out of our own way. Congratulations, my friend," Jasmine says as she offers a toast to both our new beginnings.

I take a sip of my coffee and savour its rich and complex flavour, remembering Jasmine's analogy on our first day together.

If you do not possess the undying desire to uncover your mind and soul, to dig deep within yourself, you are as useful as whole espresso beans without a grinder. You may well possess the sultriest of all worldly taste . . . but if there is no hope of releasing your flavour for consumption, there is no point in creating a space for your useless supply.

I breathe in to smell the full-bodied aroma of my coffee and know I am now deserving of my own space.

Wealth, I have come to discover, is not created or found in materialism, but in the richness of people and lies deep within each one of us. I feel an immense connection to the people here. I will never share the same blood. I could marry it; I could create it, or at least partially, but I, myself, would never be blood related, and yet I feel such a part of life here. What I have really been able to discover for myself during my time on the island is that we can choose the life we want. We can own it every day as our own—our family, our home, our love—no matter where we are or whom we are with.

There will always be a part where there is no understanding. Emotions will arise that we may never fully be able to comprehend. We can empathize with another, but we will never truly know the logic or the reason or the history or the complete depth of another's emotion or another's mind. There will be no way we will ever know exactly how another person feels, and there will be no words that will ever entirely explain this. There are moments, however, when language does not suffice, when we have to believe in more. These are the places in life where we will truly begin to know each other. We can choose to feel the pain, looking through another's eyes and through his heart, taking his suffering as our own and relating it to our own life. We can put ourselves into another's world and, through that world, we can become that person who, in turn, can become us; this is the space where real communication takes place. This is the space where the world is saved, where love is real, where there is no agenda, and where peace is all there is. When we can open our hearts to hold the burden of another at this level, even if this is only for one, single, solitary moment, it is in this moment that we choose love. It is in this moment that we are all free.

Even if we decide to reclaim the burden and the division that has previously kept us apart, and choose to go back to what we have always known to be true, we can be reassured that no matter how much we deny the truth to ourselves, the load we once carried will never be the same. A part, even if only a very small part, now knows what it is like to be free. The reasons why are incomprehensible in these moments; the understanding is irrelevant. It is only the feeling of two hearts that are completely open to each other without boundary that sets us free. I think of what my mother once said on our picnic years ago:

Rules are for needlework, not nations.

And I now understand exactly what she meant.

Since I have been here, I have come to truly know the meaning of In Lak 'ech—I am you, and you are me—and my heart has never felt more open, my head never so close to the sky and my feet never more grounded on Earth. Life is not about thinking from your head; it is about living from your heart.

∞∞∞∞∞∞

I take Jasmine's moped and make my way to the ferry. As I stand and wait for the passengers to disembark, I feel as though I am fifteen again. The anxiety in my stomach rumbles when I see Julian. I wave, and we make our way toward each other. Everything feels so familiar as if no time has passed and, yet, all seems completely unknown at the same time. I can feel him before he even touches me. He gently grabs me and squeezes me tight. I feel the curve of his back as I hug him and the smoothness of his skin, even through his shirt. I have gone far too long without him. I place my face lightly into his neck and feel home again. He leans into me and breathes deeply, without saying anything at all.

Eventually, we pull ourselves apart to speak to each other, but mention nothing of the deep rush of emotion that has us both pounding almost uncontrollably inside and barely able to stand still in front of each other.

"You shaved," I comment and smile, looking at his smooth, unblemished and practically edible skin. Well accustomed to his shaving rituals, I know his goatees disappear when he starts a new venture.

"You noticed," he responds, seductively teasing me, as he lightly rubs each side of his face with his thumb and forefinger.

"Makes for a better tan," he adds.

"Probably will," I respond.

"Figured it was time for a new project."

"Probably is," I admit.

No matter what has happened or the reasons why, he is the man who has changed my entire life. He has taken me higher and darker than I have ever been and, despite the struggle, I am deeply grateful to him. And now I have the opportunity to give him the one true source of inspiration he has spent his life wanting and forever living without—his mother.

We climb on the moped and make our way back to Jasmine's. Julian tucks his chin just over my shoulder and slightly into the curve of my neck and pulls me into him. I feel his strong arms solid around me again and honestly feel that I need nothing more in life than this very moment. A tornado of excitement spirals through me as we speed our way to the beach house. I breathe in and watch the palm trees bend with the wind, almost as if intentionally outlining our path and bowing to offer Julian his homecoming.

∞∞∞∞∞∞∞

Leaving the bags inside the entrance, Jasmine and Julian walk out to the back patio overlooking the ocean as I make my way back downtown, to give them some time alone and to wait for Dane's arrival.

After parking the moto beside the ferry terminal, I take a walk. I pass some vendors in the centro along the beach and stop to watch a man sifting through his shells and arranging the ones he will sell at his stand. His job is not much different than mine, I think. Fittingly, I see how he places the new amongst the old and strategically aligns his selection to get the sale. He smiles and nods to me.

"How do you know?" I speak out to him.

"Know what?"

"The ones that will sell," I answer.

"The gem. Ya know." He shakes his head, confidently.

"But how?"

"You know, don't ya? What do ya do?" he questions me.

"Publish books."

"What's your name?"

"Natalie Lauren."

"All right, Natalie, how do ya know what book to publish?"

"Good question," I laugh. "Look for the gem, right?"

"Yep," he says assuredly. "Everyone wants the gem. Funny thing: not many know how to see 'em and even fewer brave enough to look."

"So, how do you know?"

"You know don't ya, Natalie? You see 'em."

"But what about the ones that get chipped?" I ask.

"Gives 'em soul. Makes 'em real. Like your books. Ya want the real story, don't ya?" he smiles.

I agree with him as I notice the ferry coming into shore.

"I have to go meet my friend," I explain.

"Before ya go, take this," he says as he gestures to a small wrapped cloth.

Holding it in his hand, he unravels a glass gemstone, blue and finely chiselled on all sides.

"The blue diamond," he says. "Next time you have a hard time decidin', she'll help ya t'know." He winks at me.

I look at him as he hands me his gem, which, of course, is not a real diamond, but very beautiful nonetheless. I thank him. He grabs my hand tightly and, smiling, nods with certainty before concentrating back again on his shells.

I stand for a few moments, appreciating the beauty in humanity. Watching the shell man, I realize that when a person truly does what they love in life, there is nothing they need but that innate feeling of knowing who they are and that all is working toward the betterment of the world. We are all here to provide these little clues to each other along the way. I am grateful to just be handed another.

"Thank you," I say again and smile, before turning to make my way to meet Dane.

"Need a ride stranger?" I call out to him.

"Only if it's on the back of one of those with one of you," he teases.

"That's good, 'cause that's all I'm selling." He gives me a strong hug with his left arm and kisses the top of my forehead.

Once back at Jasmine's, Dane places his bags inside, and we head down to the beach as Jasmine and Julian continue to go through Karina's belongings in the house. I explain the occurrences of the past few days here and our discoveries of Karina and the painting, while Dane describes some of his new insights about himself and the plans for his journey.

Dane's responsibilities have continually demanded his leadership over the years and helped support him through a lot of hardship, when he had to take care of everyone else. When his father left, he promised himself that he would never allow for that type of unsettledness to happen again. So he designed a life of structure, constantly ensuring systems were held in place as a guarantee, making his word the dominating quality that defined him. What he failed to realize over the years, however, is that he was free to have it all. His mother had been sober for years, his business had never been better and, in all reality, the only obstacle that held him back now was simply his own decision.

"Did you ever play pin-the-tail-on-the-donkey when you were a kid?" Dane asks.

"Yeah, played a few times." I laugh, trying to figure out where he is possibly going with this one.

"I always cheated," he admits.

"Me too. Who didn't?"

"What were you so afraid of?" he questions me.

"Not winning?" I propose.

"But did you ever win?" he counters.

"Well, you couldn't. If you did, then everyone knew you cheated. The game was impossible," I admit.

"Exactly," he exclaims. "You'd do whatever it took to win and then pull yourself out of the running."

"Funny how you decide so young what's important and how much you're willing to gamble to maintain the facade, but won't actually risk the uncertainty to do what it takes to win," I conclude.

"And amazing," he emphasizes, "how fast childhood games quickly become business alliances and vicious circles in life."

"Never risk too much, for fear of losing."

"Never excel, for fear of ridicule," Dane replies, explaining the real reason he had limited himself to such guarded frameworks.

"And always playing a game you're never going to win," I add.

"Nate, I'm makin' up a new game," Dane says as he places his hand on the back of my neck and pulls me into him, hugging my shoulder.

"Barnett, it's about time," I respond, breathing in his familiar cologne as I pull my arm tight around him. And I agree with him, the time has come for both of us to throw in all our blindfolds and old foam mallets.

We sit in silence, watching the birds now flying overhead.

"What kind of a bird's that?" Dane questions, looking at the large black and white bird soaring above us.

"Fricataus. Amazing, isn't it? Doesn't use its wings. Just lets the wind dictate its direction. Harmony, balance. Stays open to the path."

"Trust. Now there's a concept, Nate," he teases.

I grab Dane's arm from around my neck and smooth his hand between my palms.

"Barnett . . . have I ever told you, you're my best friend?"

"Trust ya with my life, girl," he responds.

Our bond is for life, and we both know it. Nothing and no one will ever come between us, through love and hate, peace and war, we are family for each other. We are one.

We head back up to the house to join the others.

∞∞∞∞∞∞∞

Once inside, I introduce Jasmine to Dane and then go to join Julian, who is now standing in front of his painting in the hallway.

"Remember the day," he says quietly as I stand beside him.

"Tell me," I request, wanting now to hear the real beginning.

Julian re-creates the conversation between himself and his mother.

You have a gift, Julian.

What if they don't like my pictures?

Paint with all your heart. Never hide anything. There's a way to the world. Don't fight what's real. Believe. What you have, Julian, the world needs. You may have to work to convince people, but always be honest with yourself.

Julian enters the bedroom and sits down in the chair beside the bed and asks me if I know how long it's been that he has done just the opposite. I watch, still wondering what his secrets are, but refrain from prying. I suddenly feel as if the conversation we had that first night together is about to reconvene and go to the depths that I had originally hoped it would. Julian reaches for the teak box of Karina's belongings that Jasmine has left for him on the bed and pulls an old leather journal from its collection.

"I know there's still some stuff between us, but—"

"I know," I interrupt.

I have forgiven him and feel that what needs to work itself out will. This is about Karina now. And I want to know everything.

"I'd like to—" he starts and motions toward the journal.

"I'd like that too."

Opening the journal, Julian begins to read Karina's earliest entry as I lie down on the bed, soon to understand the commitment of a mother and the heart of a young dancing gypsy.

> *Anger, others controlling my destiny, I will not accept. I will fight. Optimism, integrity, individuality, drive—these I will embrace. I will not be driven down. I am free and I will fight for my freedom to live. I am alive. I will not be smothered with the dark cloak of negativity, by anyone. I will shake all I need to, to push forward. I will move toward a positive light. I will march on. I will stand against my odds and win. I am ready to listen and allow my destiny to lead me forward. I am ready to hear the voice within. I will allow myself to be directed. I will follow. I will forever will my love to my son. He will hear my spirit. He will know my song. And in the end, he, too, will sing.*

She never left. She never gave up and she continually kept Julian with her. The difference between her and me is that she refused to be controlled by the anger. She accepted her circumstance, to learn the lessons she needed to master. In spite of everything, she freely chose to accept her life, to stand for her son and discover the future, having no attachment to its outcome and holding only the faith that it would all eventually work out.

Julian fumbles through the box in front of him and pulls out a picture of his father, young and happy, and another one of himself with his mother, lying nestled in bed, a snapshot his father had obviously taken of the two sound asleep, heads resting on their pillows and arms stretched above their heads. Julian fights tears and admits to his anger, and his wonder, about a life that could have been completely different.

After several minutes, he returns to Karina's journal and continues.

I hear the leaves gently blow in the damp night air. Walking on the path, through the trees, I am at home and safe. Along this lush trail, I come to swirl round in a circle, flipping my dress into the air and announcing, "Tonight, I am a dancer, world-famous and wonderful. I am Karina." They allow me to be as flamboyant and dramatic as I dare, these trees. They do not judge or conform. They giggle at my extravagance. I entertain and provide them diversion from their long, blistering day. Although I entered saddened, they bring me alive. I breathe in their renewal and release my day. In adoration I run into their arms each night and fill myself with their peace. I silently blow my sweet kisses, remembering a time when I was free, full of love and discovery.

Julian smiles at me.

"Trees." He laughs. "Big theme."

"Family thing." I smile and wink at him, knowing the special connection that he feels with his mother and just wishing I could have discovered this information a year or two earlier.

Julian finds an envelope addressed to him and sits frozen now, almost in horror, staring at an unforeseen conversation with his mother. Understanding the reason for her abandonment is one thing, but having the courage to read his dead mother's words written directly to him is completely another. I watch him, wondering what it could possibly be like to travel his lifetime without her and now have her unspoken words in his hand.

He sits silent for several minutes, bracing his forehead with his hand, with his thumb and middle finger held lightly on each temple. Reaching forward, I gently pull the envelope from his other hand as he lifts his face from his fingers to look at me. Quietly, I open its seal, extracting the letter and slowly begin to deliver a dead mother's ultimate gift to her son, astounded at how such a simple letter could make life seem so alive and real once again.

My dearest Julian,

It is through my suffering I have learned. I have been fortunate, for this has granted me the lessons that have given me my life. The only experience I have missed is you, my son. You should know, however, you have travelled each and every day with me. I have taken you with me everywhere and still remember your smell and your laughter. Knowing this, and truly believing me, you will know you have everything you need. Just as you have been the greatest gift of my life, you, in return, have the greatest to give.

Be strong in the face of fear. Julian, you are a man of many talents. Through the years these may have been thwarted or challenged in one way or another. This is only so that you may learn to concentrate on your truest talent. Love, Julian. In the face of fear, love.

There was a time in my life when I, too, thought this never possible. Your father taught me different. He was the one man, in my entire life, who was able to see me. Julian, he understood and loved me deeply. You were created out of passion, out of love, out of magic. Our moments were magical, my son, as you are. In the face of fear, Julian, love. Love is where you will find your magic. Nothing will ever be bigger than this. Nothing will ever be better.

I met her many years ago, gave her a reading along the beach. She knows me as Sofia. Remind her. She is the one, Julian. Do not be afraid. She understands you. She loves you. You can hear each other. Her magic has brought you to me. Do not be afraid, now, to let go. You have made your journey. You have searched and found, and there is *nothing left to find. There is nothing but the love of the heart. People will accept this or deny it, but one day it will all be real. Only fear consumes, Julian. The extraordinary reach beyond it, my son.*

Reach. Live your love.

I sit back in shock, trying to fathom and possibly comprehend what I have just read.

"You met her?" Julian asks, now completely dumbfounded.

"Apparently. After your opening, when we first met, I made a trip to the Caribbean. There was a fortune teller at the restaurant there. Her name was Sofia."

"And you talked to her?"

"She gave me a reading. I cannot believe she was your mother." I pause, thinking back. "So, that's why," I say, talking to myself.

"What's why?"

I can hear the urgency in Julian's voice and am quick to explain. "She never let me pay her. I couldn't understand. Eman told me I would, that Sofia saw magic. Didn't make any sense to me."

"You pay for that kind of thing?"

"Usually," I reply.

"You said the trip was just after my opening?"

"Yeah."

"Fuck." Julian exhales slowly, shaking his head.

"What?" I question.

"I was there. I was that close."

"What do you mean, you were there? You were in Paris."

"No, I wasn't. I was there."

"I don't get it."

"I'm not who you think I am, Natalie. There's a lot you don't know."

FIFTEEN

And the day came when the risk it took to remain tight in a bud was more painful than the risk it took to blossom.

— Anaïs Nin

"I was young then and broke. I was also too naïve to understand the implications or the complicated criminal world I was entering," Julian admits as he begins to explain the twisted situation he got himself involved in years ago to finance his first studio in New York, around the same time he had first met Dane.

"Bougain's the guy. I'd do some paintings. He'd give me a whack of cash then resell the paintings."

"Legitimately?"

"Not exactly," he says, squinting his face with a slight grimace.

"He had a whole scam, smuggling through the Caribbean. On the cruise ships."

"Jesus, Julian. Who is this guy?"

"He was at my studio the night of the opening."

"Don't even tell me," I say as I lift my palm in a halting motion. "The older guy, tall, slick, wore a bracelet on his wrist, with some kind of medallion on it?" I question, knowing exactly who he means.

"Yeah, that's him."

"I saw him on that trip."

"No doubt; he had a hand-off that same week. I was down there to give him the painting."

"Why didn't you tell me?"

"Nate, believe me. I couldn't get you involved."

"No. Much better to throw it all away," I say facetiously.

"Till I got myself sorted out, yeah it was," he says, defending his decision.

"So, you're telling me you're through?"

"Yep."

"You're sure?"

"Done."

"Does Dane know?"

"No."

"Eman?"

"No. No one," he confirms.

He sits in the armchair across from me with his arms folded behind his head and Karina's journal in his lap. I stare directly into his eyes. I look over every ounce of his skin, knowing his familiarity and, yet, questioning whether I can believe him. I know I cannot forgive him only halfway. The difficulty is accepting the lies and knowing how capable he is of deception. It means letting go of the devastating feeling of exclusion I felt when he left, of being alone and betrayed. It means trusting him from here and not blaming.

After several minutes of envisioning every possible, probable or even slightly imaginable future, I admit that I am no different. My withholdings were not about art dealers and replicas but I, too, had hidden a great deal. I can accept the past as just that now and put it away. And Karina had been right: I cannot judge Julian's actions, for I, too, have made my own mistakes.

Breaking the silence, Julian slowly reopens Karina's journal and quietly asks if we can continue. I nod.

Lifting a ballet ticket from a place that marks her final entry, Julian pulls the small ticket stub out and begins to read the last few moments of his mother's life.

> *Tonight, Jasmine and I attended the final performance I will see. I am not well. I watched and recalled the many times I danced for Adrian, and the times we spent as lovers, so many years ago. My dance is now over, I know.*
>
> *I stood in the restroom in the theatre tonight behind a young girl, watching her reflection in the mirror. Her skin was brilliant. I paled drastically in comparison, with the darkened circles beneath my eyes. For the first time, I saw my years of experience. I saw my age. I am no*

longer a young face. Time has passed, suddenly, without notice.

As I re-entered the lobby, I straightened myself and pulled my shawl across my shoulders and made my way through the crowd back to Jasmine. I had come a long way in this life. I was not giving up now. Others watched. Even in my weakened strength, I am still strong and determined. Others smiled as I smiled back. I looked amongst the people, but did not see him. I had prayed over the years I would see Julian in a crowd similar to this. I had hoped life would grant me one opportunity to see him again, just one chance, to brush past my son, as a man. I would not even need to utter a sound, merely brush his arm in a crowd of strangers. He would know me no different from another but, for me, my life would be complete. I had only asked for the one glimpse. I was aware now it would not come to pass.

The performance was brilliant. There is a feeling in the heart of a dancer that never leaves, that never wanes. Circumstances arrive, but the heart is forever filled with movement and its lesson. I am thankful for my dance and for my song.

From the documents Jasmine has compiled, Julian and I soon discover the events following her last entry. The next morning, Karina was found in a large wicker chair in the middle of her backyard garden. Alone and amongst lush greenery, she sat with a wooden box of all her favourite possessions at her feet, with a small velvet ribbon draped across her knee and the insignia of the Black Madonna still clasped in her hand.

The coroner's research reported one unexplainable mystery, however, as a single leaf was found in her mouth. Logistically, this would not have been impossible, as she died in the midst of a forested area. A leaf could have easily fallen from the trees. Karina was found, however, with her head bowed. The leaf revealed, after later forensic analysis, that it had been extracted from its original branch over thirty-five years ago and was not indigenous to this region of Mexico at all.

The Maya believe trees are our connection between the physical and the spiritual worlds; essential to life, they are our link to enlightenment. Like the tree, once we can become grounded and centred in our own roots, we can become healthy and flexible enough to change, and free to give ourselves to others. To go back up the tree of life is to return to the divine and to the purest light. Our whole purpose is to get back to our pure essence. It is true: Karina had come full circle, and she had left all Julian would ever need to also find his own way.

Julian smoothes the velvet ribbon between his hands, knowing it as the same one he and his mother had carefully wrapped around a willow branch so many years ago. Death could take her very life, but Karina would continue to hold strong for her son, even in her death planting the familiar reminders, so that he would eventually find the truth.

Closing his mother's journal and the many gaps in his own life, Julian carefully places all of her belongings back into their box and turns to face me directly.

Never could I have even imagined that the individual struggles that so dramatically wedged us apart would be the same that would eventually bring us together. With no more avoidance, no more hiding and no more secrets, I have found my musician, a man who can hear the song within his heart and inspire mine.

"Well, Ms. Lauren, you've certainly outdone yourself this time," Julian says as he crawls onto the bed with me.

I smirk at him in complete disbelief, proud of my accomplishment and thankful for every experience that has worked to get us here. Julian pulls me close to him and holds my face between his hands.

His breath feels warm and soothing as he whispers gently into my mouth, "What is it you want, Natalie Lauren?"

I smile. "Oh my God, Julian. You," I answer without a question in my mind.

He grabs me and pulls me into him as we rest silently together. The waiting is over. My life is here. My life is finally here, and I have everything I need to step forward.

Much later that evening, while Julian and Dane head to bed, I finish packing the last of my work and lie down for a few minutes on the sofa in the living room as Jasmine sits up at the wooden table on the patio outside and writes the foreword to Karina's story.

∞∞∞∞∞∞∞∞∞∞

A young woman could have never known the effect she would have dancing alone in her room, naked in front of a mirror. Stepping regardless of fear or apprehension, she allowed herself the space and the freedom to feel, to be. She did not force another to understand her movement, but inspired others to feel her grace and the ease in being true to oneself.

An old woman would never know that the simple love she held for her child and her lover would not only provide all they would ever need to survive, but that her story would also go on to inspire an entire nation. She was one woman who held to her dream fearlessly, never failing to step forward. She was a woman who listened to her song when no one else could hear, and provided a rhythm we would no longer want to live without. It was but a moment in time and a space within life, where one person stood and commanded the freedom and passion and power to be alive, in spite of all that existed.

In one moment, one woman sacrificed all that she had and all that she would ever know, for the sake of the dance. In the end, this would mean that we would all have the means to be free.

∞∞∞∞∞∞∞∞∞∞

I open my eyes as Jasmine enters the room.

"Finished," she says. "Tucked it in your briefcase."

"Great." I smile as I lean over on my side, and she sits down on the floor in front of me.

"No more waiting, I guess." The words linger in the air.

"Couple of months," I assure her as she bites her lip.

"It's like it's not real," she says as a tear drips down the side of her face.

"I know." I lift my hand and wipe her cheek.

"Kept believin'; just never thought about how I'd feel when it happened."

"She'll still be with you. You know that."

"Yeah, it's just letting go."

"Yeah, I know. You taught me a lot about that," I acknowledge as I reach for her hand.

"I'll leave the windows open tonight, so you get that last bit of ocean air and a nice big kiss from Ixchel," she responds.

"Thank you." I smile. "Really. Thank you for everything."

"Packed a li'l breakfast for you. Some of Don Fernando's best pears." We both smile as she whispers and winks at me. "Make sure that man of yours gets one."

"Absolutely," I confirm as she turns and walks out of the room.

Lying with my face now on the cushion, I watch her move across the tile floor and see her bare feet leave and realize that, at this point, Jasmine is my young maiden, the very same Sofia described to me on the beach a few years ago. She is the one who was waiting to walk beside me so I could learn how to feel.

Karina planted her last crop within Jasmine. Jasmine tended her seed. Now I am responsible to bring forth the message. I have spent my entire life looking for the truth, the story to define me, and here it is. I am the carrier now, the medium to portray the unleashing. I have travelled to the depths of my own humanity, cast myself to the bottom of the cavern, repeatedly, to understand the pain, the struggle, the fear and the strength that it takes to move beyond. Now I can authentically deliver, so that others will be inspired and know they are not alone. As I make my way to bed, I catch a glance of myself in the round mirror in the hallway and step back to look deeply. I see my small, young girl standing there. She has been waiting, smiling with her fingers pressed on the glass and eager now to join me, once again. I raise my palm and reconnect with hers. Tomorrow we will leave and start our new adventure, together. I lift and place a kiss on my fingers and lightly place it softly on her cheek and confirm we are never alone. I make my way to bed.

∞∞∞∞∞∞∞∞∞∞

The next morning, Dane, Julian and I bid Jasmine farewell and board the ferry. Dane will travel with us to the mainland and then set out on his way, and Julian and I will return home. We all sit along the side of the boat near the front, setting our sights on the shore ahead.

With no idea of what the next moment will bring, I sit, excited, with no compulsion to control or to understand. I have discovered the secret of my vision here, realizing now how much I have been committed to the struggle instead of the search, to looking outside instead of within, all the while not realizing that my answer did not exist in another, but within myself and my own heart. Karina had known this secret—for her it was the dance, and finding the courage to step forward, to take the stage without audience, without encouragement, for the sole reason of dancing.

In experiencing Ixchel's storms and the chance for rebirth, I have learned that accomplishment comes with unleashing the past, acknowledging its contribution and celebrating its release. If I could have known how much I had been bound by my own history, I might have freed myself long ago but, as with Karina, my lessons have granted me my life. And I know now that any attempt to avoid understanding is like pretending a small grain of sand left unattended on a hot afternoon walk, or an ugly night at the beach left unacknowledged, would never cause pain. All is eventually revealed.

Release is only granted when discovery is sought; paintings are recovered when the storm is endured. Families are found when the dance is played out, and lives are saved when you can love beyond fear. Success is not about holding or maintaining a solid sense of security, but about the ability to have faith and take great risks. Yes, one has to journey, venture, reach, find, fight and trust. One has to believe, even in times of no evidence, or of too much. There is a light on every journey, a blue diamond waiting to be found. The process, the real access to this, is not about repetitive climbs out of blackened caves or bottomless glasses of Bombay gin on the rocks; it's about courage and truth, about being able to accept the darkness and the entirety of oneself.

The wind moves gently around us as we make our way across the water. Julian sits beside me, cradling my hand in his lap as Dane sits in the row in front of us. I finish the last drop of my water before slipping the empty bottle under my arm and into my handbag. Julian, still looking forward and without even conscious thought, hands me his. I lean into him and snuggle my chin on his shoulder.

New beginnings only lie in the decision to move forward, in the choice to be willing. Finally realizing that I truly get to choose these moments, I can now create a whole new life I want to live. These new beginnings are inspiring, and beginning to love can change your entire life. But the moment—the moment of truly trusting yourself and that one unknown step into the magical blue—that, I now know, is everything.

I had come to this island jaded and worn and tired of the life I had created for myself. With the help of Jasmine, Karina and Ixchel, I trusted and took one unfamiliar step. I buried my mother and my brother and a past that no longer served me. I rediscovered my father, a family and a heart I had long lived without. I found a writer and a story and a painting but, most importantly, the diamond within myself.

Julian reaches his arm around me and holds me warmly against his side. I lean and rest with him, thankful for quiet mornings on the ocean, for life's difficult lessons and for one Julian Miras, painter of the willow and son of a great dancing gypsy.

There is a diamond buried deep within every rough

Those of patience shall discover its existence

Those of understanding shall know its worth

But only those of true and absolute beauty

Only those of unyielding strength

Venturing vacant of fear

Shall ever be rewarded the undying warmth

Of its eternal shine

—pdb, 2012

ABOUT THE AUTHOR

Penny D. Burnham is a Canadian writer who was born with the heart of a gypsy and a great sense of adventure. From a small village in Eastern Ontario, she grew up understanding the value of family, the importance of connection, and how our experiences and friendships intermingle to teach us all so many great lessons in life.

With a passion for lifelong learning, a BA in gerontology and sociology, several years of extended studies in communication and leadership training, and a few entrepreneurial ventures of her own, Penny has worked many years in small business development and administration within a variety of industries in Canada and Mexico, including: aviation, business coaching, education, finance, healthcare, hospitality, tourism, mining, oil and gas. Her previous published works include: operational, procedural and production manuals; training program modules; website copy and marketing materials; technical user guides; and poetry.

Initially intrigued by the Mayan culture through her own research, Penny discovered Isla Mujeres in 1998 and eventually, in 2006, with only the belongings she could fit into a suitcase, moved to live on the island for five years. Fulfilling a lifelong dream of following her passion for writing and insatiable love for Mexico and its people, she immersed herself into its magical culture and the true Mexican way of life. Her first novel, *Jaded Diamond,* empowers us all to see beyond the limits of our minds and egos, to break down the barriers separating who we have become from who we really are, and to discover what is truly possible.

Currently, Penny lives in Eastern Ontario, travels internationally, and is working on her next great adventure.